LIFE:
FOUR QUARTERS
PLUS OVERTIME

TO: Jessica,
Your dedication shapes lives and futures every single day.
Life is "Super Fanfabulous"

God bless!

[signature] 10, 2025

LIFE:
FOUR QUARTERS PLUS OVERTIME

FLOYD L. GRIFFIN JR.

Library of Congress Control Number: 2019914920
ISBN: Hardcover   978-1-7960-6155-0
                   Softcover   978-1-7960-6154-3
                   eBook   978-1-7960-6153-6

Scripture quotations marked KJV are from the Holy Bible, King James Version (Authorized Version). First published in 1611. Quoted from the KJV Classic Reference Bible, Copyright © 1983 by The Zondervan Corporation.

Scripture quotations marked NASB are taken from the New American Standard Bible®, Copyright © 1960, 1962, 1963, 1968, 1971, 1972, 1973, 1975, 1977, 1995 by The Lockman Foundation. Used by permission.

Scripture quotations marked NIV are taken from the Holy Bible, New International Version®. NIV®. Copyright © 1973, 1978, 1984 by International Bible Society. Used by permission of Zondervan. All rights reserved. [Biblica]

Scripture quotations are from the ESV® Bible (The Holy Bible, English Standard Version®), copyright © 2001 by Crossway, a publishing ministry of Good News Publishers. Used by

Any people depicted in stock imagery provided by Getty Images are models, and such images are being used for illustrative purposes only.
Certain stock imagery © Getty Images.

Print information available on the last page.

Rev. date: 10/03/2019

To order additional copies of this book, contact:
Xlibris
1-888-795-4274
www.Xlibris.com
Orders@Xlibris.com
794198

This book is dedicated to my family members and the Tuskegee University, all of whom impacted my life so profoundly.

My beautiful wife of fifty-three years, Nathalie Huffman Griffin, who is my best friend and the mother of my children, you have been a rock for me all these years. From the second quarter to our overtime together, I am the man I am because of you.

My parents, Floyd L. Griffin Sr. and Ruth Evans Griffin, though you have both gone home to be with the Lord, you were there for me from the first through the fourth quarters, giving me the foundation for a good life and preparing me to pass on your love and wisdom to my own children.

Tuskegee University—our alma mater, where I met and married Nathalie and where both our sons and one grandson are alumni—you played such an important role in the man I grew into. I received my second lieutenant commission in the US Army, learned about the civil rights movement, became an activist while at Tuskegee, and later, got inducted into the ROTC Hall of Fame. Nathalie and I created a Tuskegee family–endowed scholarship, and I faithfully served on the trustee board for several years. I cannot overstate your importance in our lives. May you continue to be a guiding force of achievement for future generations as you have been for the Griffin family.

How far you go in life depends on your being tender with the young, compassionate with the aged, sympathetic with the striving, and tolerant of the weak and strong. Because someday in your life you will have been all of these.

—George Washington Carver

CONTENTS

FOREWORD

Floyd Griffin's book entitled *Life – Four Quarters Plus Overtime* is such a powerful and informative tool for not only the African-American community, but humanity.

I have known Floyd for over 16 years. In those years he has inspired me in my political and civil rights career. Floyd is a motivator who will captivate you, inspire you and inform you in his new book. It is an educational and informative read that will leave you thinking creatively by motivating you to discover your own personal power from within. Floyd's passion for civic engagement and business acumen has been a resource and example for many people. Dr. Martin Luther King's dream still to this day touches millions of people around the globe, but if we don't continue to fight, dream, talk about, discuss and imagine, the dream of Dr. King will slip away.

As the national president and CEO of the Southern Christian Leadership Conference (SCLC), the organization co-founded by Dr. Martin Luther King, Jr., I believe in always checking the scales of injustice. This is the book to help us all check the scales as we seek to make Dr. King's dream a reality.

Charles Steele, Jr.

National President and CEO

320 Auburn Avenue Atlanta, GA 30303— www.nationalsclc.org — (404) 522-1420 office— (404) 527-4333 fax

Dr. Charles Steele, President/CEO, Southern Christian Leadership Conference (SCLC)

INTRODUCTION

*God and nature first made us what we are and then out
of our own created genius we make ourselves what we
want to be. Follow always that great law. Let the sky and
God be our limit and eternity our measurement.*

—Marcus Mosiah Garvey Jr.,
Jamaican-born black nationalist and president general of the
Universal Negro Improvement Association and
African Communities League

I had just conducted a funeral for a woman who passed away in her late eighties. As the minister was concluding his eulogy, he shared with the family and friends in attendance that she had lived a long and full life, reached an age qualifying her as an elder, and had entered the "overtime" before she succumbed.

In my role as funeral director, I conducted thousands of funeral or memorial services, but at that specific moment, the notion of the "overtime" hit me like a ton of bricks. It felt like a spiritual reawakening. It occurred to me that this person had lived seventy-plus years, so something monumental had to have occurred before these moments of solemn reflections and tearful remembrances. Time after time, this thought kept coming back to me.

The Bible says in Psalm 90:10 New American Standard, "As for the days of your life, they contain seventy years [which is equivalent to three scores plus ten] or if due to strength, eighty years."

When I did the calculations, I realized that the span of our life could be divided into quarters—conception through early adolescence (ages zero to seventeen), late adolescence through early adulthood (ages eighteen to thirty-five), midlife (ages thirty-six to fifty-two), and late adulthood (ages fifty-three to seventy) with the overtime (age seventy-plus)—representing when we're most inspired to evaluate the sum total of our lives. This has continued to be a theme that I explore again and again, as I, at the age of seventy-five, journey through my own "overtime."

I have been blessed to have a good and successful existence with my life partner, Nathalie, who I've been happily wedded to for over fifty-three years, grown sons with and a goddaughter who have achieved acclaim in their own right juggling the added responsibility of family and kids. I've served as an ROTC cadet, Vietnam helicopter pilot, army colonel, college football coach, professor, businessman, state senator, author, and mayor. I never dreamed all these could or would be possible.

From childhood to mature adulthood, I was empowered to observe my parents, Floyd L. Griffin Sr. and Ruth Evans Griffin—both God-fearing Christians, loving, present, and purposeful in all their endeavors. Maintaining active involvement in the community and success in their many business ventures, consistently employing humility, stability, and courageousness were their trademarks.

I understood it to be my duty to pass on the human dignity my parents had consistently reflected.

So you see, my success is not mine alone. It represents all their passion, joy, and pain, the prayers petitioned on bent knees, the sound guidance and sacrifices, and the unceasing faithfulness of my village of extended family and friends.

Life: Four Quarters plus Overtime is a gift I give lovingly for all God has given me. Writing this book isn't something I pulled out of thin air. The Lord put it in my heart to create it specifically with the African American community in mind. Oh, that this book would touch and heal our wounded places and set us free to manifest our divine destiny.

In the course of this book, we will examine the periods of development associated with the human life span with brief overviews of the social, emotional, cognitive, perceptual, and moral development specific to each life stage. For example, having productive (early adulthood to midlife) quarter takes extensive planning, setting and achieving goals, and having the wherewithal and courage to move to the next level—thinking analytically and acting strategically while maintaining a vision of the ultimate destination.

The book will include cutting-edge commentary from experts in the fields of psychology, public health, education, religion, gerontology, and the healing arts. Each quarter will have African proverbs, cultural maxims, quotes, stories, words of wisdom from black achievers, along with biblical scripture that will strengthen our faith and belief and help us interpret (and experience) our lives in a vastly different way.

> *Out of the wombs of a frail world new systems*
> *of justice and equality are being born.*
>
> —Rev. Martin Luther King Jr.,
> *Beyond Vietnam: A Time to Break the Silence,*
> Riverside Church, April 4, 1967

African Americans can no longer languish in the margins in a country that is ours by birth. We must claim our inheritance by taking the corrective measures necessary to delete the programmed mind-set and heal the trauma associated with post-traumatic slavery syndrome (PTSS). This is the work.

Life: Four Quarters plus Overtime is a call to action to arm ourselves with knowledge of our ancient history; rectify the miseducation our children have been subjected to; restore the social justice identity of our religious institutions; honor the intelligence, wisdom, and personal power of our elders; lift up our sons and daughters as influential leaders in the making, thereby gaining full access to our "silver rights" and the economic democracy Reverend King so eloquently spoke of.

For I know the plans I have for you," declares the Lord, "plans to prosper you, and not to harm you, plans to give you hope, and a future."

—Jeremiah 29:11 New International Version

It is my desire that *Life—Four Quarters Plus Overtime* will empower you to see yourself in the context of a greater whole, thereby activating the rudiments of the mind of God that is within you. Like the mighty oak tree within the tiny acorn, everything that you are and all you could ever hope to be is already deeply embedded within you. With our physical, emotional, and spiritual intelligence intact, we can rebuild our sacred geometry—one woman, one man, one child, and one "come-unity" at a time for the benefit of planet Earth as a whole.

No matter your age or the quarter you are currently in, I implore you to read *Life: Four Quarters plus Overtime* and create a *pledge* (personalized with your family's surname) to recommit yourself to life so that you and your loved ones may experience the best versions of yourselves, *here* and *now.*

Think of this as an invitation.

DEFINING HUMAN DEVELOPMENT

For you formed my inward parts, you knitted me together in my mother's womb. I praise you, for I am fearfully and wonderfully made. Wonderful are your works, my soul knows it very well.

—Psalm 139:13–15 English Standard Version

The recitation of Psalm 139 * New International Version emanates a sublime, delicate, and divine sensation that stirs us to contemplate the intricately woven depths of God's creations. His engagement in our lives magnificently transcends all knowing.

God, you molded my unformed substance in secret and authored the book in which the days that were fashioned for me were inscribed. Your greatness touches each and every aspect of my life. You understand my thoughts and remain acquainted with all my ways. Nothing can separate me from your hand of love and tender care. You see all there is and know the reason for everything. I can never be hidden from you. Oh, that I might comprehend the composition of your miracles and mysteries.

With knowledge, you bless your children all the days of our lives. I ride on the wings of the morning with you and dwell by distant shores. Even in those hidden places, your hand guides me, and your strength supports me.

Your concern for all creation commences at conception. In your Word (*Logos*) are the instructions that we must adhere to, to be caretakers of the seed you planted in the receptacle (the womb) in which all human life takes shape and grows.

---

* Excerpts from Psalm 139: 1–16 rewritten to identify the Word (*Logos*) as the source of our initial understanding of human development.

Heavenly Father, it is within your infinite power and wisdom that the structure of our bodies are manifested, bequeathing all manner of wonder and astonishment. Our inner embellishment is a network of organs, bones, muscles, connective tissue, veins, and arteries, a holographic projection of consciousness, all framed and designed with exquisite skill.

We keep at the forefront of our collective mind an inner awareness that you, God, will direct our path on this brief earthly sojourn. Our African foremothers and forefathers were well-versed in your ways, recognizing with reverence your supremacy as the Most High God, creator of the world. Those ancestors, heroes, and historical figures adhered to customs and morally sound behavior understanding the causal agency of the universe and its interrelationships with the human race.

You blessed us with ancestors whose well-defined life plan specifically included each stage of human development from conception to the afterlife. African rites of passage that occur throughout the life span typically at birth, marriage, and death, during initiations and upon achieving an important position or milestone. Those life cycle rituals and ceremonies are infused with cultural, spiritual, and psychological significance representing the transition from one social or religious status to another.

Contemporary concepts of human development take into account the theories, observations, research, and personal histories gleaned from developmental psychologists, psychiatrists, and other social scientists whose work has shaped this relatively new scientific discipline. Social scientists continue to play an integral role in the study of human development. And like the phases it examines and the developmentalists themselves, change, evolution, and growth are a constant.

Researcher and educator Joy DeGruy is restoring the spiritual/mental/physical wholeness of those whose ancestors withstood the Maafa (the African Holocaust) in her landmark scholarship on post-traumatic slavery syndrome (PTSS), a condition that exists as a consequence of the multigenerational oppression of Africans and their descendants via chattel slavery and the institutional racism associated with America's legacy of enduring trauma and subjugation. Her work inspires others to be the healing, the balm in the Gilead, those soul revivors who will transmute and restore our stolen legacy.

Developmental psychologist and psychoanalyst Erik Erikson theorized that development functions via the epigenetic principle, a predetermined unfolding of our personalities, which occur within the context of relationships with parents, siblings, friends, and community. His work also examined the interaction of generations, which he called mutuality, and the ways in which our lives intermesh. Each stage (from infancy to end of life) involves specific developmental tasks that are psychosocial in nature. Successful completion of one stage leads to the acquisition and mastery of specific skills, attitudes, and beliefs that assist one in navigating the tasks of the next stage.

During each of the eight psychosocial developmental stages, there is a psychological conflict or crisis that must be resolved. One of the strengths of Erikson's theory is its ability to tie together important psychosocial development across the entire life span. Erickson's own quest for identity and the need to redefine it reflected the identity crisis (a term he coined) that he faced as a young immigrant and later observed in World World II combat soldiers and members of disenfranchised minority groups.

Psychologist G. Stanley Hall's pioneering work was devoted to the study of childhood, adolescence, and aging. He observed that males tend to have an increase in sensation seeking and aggression during adolescence with a corresponding increase in criminal activity during that life span. Hall noted that there were two types of aggression: the relational aggression associated with gossiping, rumor spreading, exclusion of others, which is more prevalent in females, and physical aggression, which occurs more often in males. He founded this theory on an understanding of the nature of childhood, suggesting that only a reformed system of education could ensure children matured into healthy, productive, adult members of society. Much of Hall's understanding of human development still holds true today even though most was gleaned from 1890 to 1905 at the height of his influential work in child studies.

Psychiatrist and hospice pioneer Elisabeth Kübler-Ross's groundbreaking book *On Death and Dying* (published in 1969) and near-death studies formed what is known as the Kübler-Ross model, which identifies the patterns of adjustment represented in the five stages of grief. Her work provides genuine insights and empathetic depictions of the social, emotional, and spiritual world of the dying and their loved ones. Fifty years after its publication, Kübler-Ross's book continues to stimulate conversations on the ethical and social dilemmas we face as we seek to accept dying and death with dignity.

Psychologist Jean Piaget is known for his scholarship in child development. His curiosity and creative inquiries inspired much of what we know about the way children think. Piaget applied his extensive knowledge of biology, philosophy, and psychology in his observations and conversations with his own youngsters and other children, thereby forming his complex theories about cognitive development, which occurs as a result of biological maturation and interaction with the environment. Cognitive development represents the changes in the child's thought process that facilitate a growing ability to acquire and utilize knowledge about their world. Like Hall, Piaget placed great importance on the proper education of children, stating that "only education is capable of saving our societies from possible collapse, whether violent or gradual."

It is through the collective scholarship of these (and other) social scientists that we can now define the complexities and predictability of this process of human development, its continuity, and its physical, cognitive, and social influences.

Infinite potentiality exists within each of us, as we constantly die and are reborn, from moment to moment, literally transforming at the molecular level, for example, every three days a new stomach lining, every thirty-five days a new outer layer of skin (epidermis), every three months a new skeleton, and every year an almost entirely new body.

From the most dire of circumstances, we can emerge fully whole, relishing the once-invisible future that has come into fruition. The growth and changes that occur in infancy and early childhood can be replicated as intuition, intellect, and imagination are implicit no matter one's age, that is, the synthesis of knowledge and experience into wisdom.

Each aspect of development whether physical, intellectual, spiritual, or social affects the other. When tallied collectively, we see the impact it can have on future development and the individuated change, growth, and evolution that is critical to the process.

Periods of the Life Span

For the purpose of this book, we have divided the human life span into four quarters plus overtime. Therefore, the age divisions are estimated and not exact representations of the social, emotional, and physical criteria that signals the shift from one developmental period to the next.

The First Quarter—Conception through Early Adolescence (Age 0–17)

> *Infants descend from the stars and are still*
> *listening to the Music of the Spheres.*
>
> —Hazrat Inayat Khan, Sufi teacher

Prepare to care; life is emerging. A sperm cell and an ovum fuse. An embryo mysteriously transforms into a fetus (Latin for "bringing forth") nine weeks later. The amniotic sac envelopes the fetus in a translucent liquid cushion made up of 98 percent water and 2 percent cells and salts.

The amniotic sac, the placenta (a pancake-shaped organ attached to the inside of the uterus) and the umbilical cord (a lifeline conjoining the placenta to the fetus) represent the fetal life-support arsenal.

At five months, the brain of a fetus has more nerve connections than that of an adult, though true brain life begins in the weeks just prior to birth. The growth that initially occurred via cell division has now differentiated into billions of cells, each with specified functions. A positive birth experience has immense psychological significance challenging the mother-to-be to grow and change in life-expanding ways. What occurs in the womb has an influential impact on every aspect of our external life experiences.

A woman giving birth to a child has pain because her time
has come; but when her baby is born she forgets her anguish
because of her joy that a child is born into the world.

—John 16:21 New International Version

One of the most crucial stages of human development begins in the first one and a half to two years of life. Many milestones are achieved during this life stage as infants gain mastery over their bodies. Each newly mastered skill prepares them to undertake the next in a preordained sequence that provides opportunities to explore and manipulate their environment and experience sensory and cognitive stimulation. Infants form attachments to their parents, siblings, and other caregivers, creating the sense of security that's needed if they are to develop both physically and emotionally. Children, particularly those ages two to four, operate at the genius level, experiencing and seeing the world through a spiritual lens. Matthew 18:1–5 New International Version alludes to their fundamental goodness and the prominent place they hold in the kingdom of heaven.

We desire to bequeath two things to our children;
the first one is roots, the other one is wings.

—Sudanese proverb

Early childhood is a dreamlike time of inventiveness and imaginative exploration, a period in which rich and diverse images, feelings, perceptions, and systems of belief emerge. Children become progressively independent, learning increasingly advanced skills and capabilities as they grow older. Their heightened sense of self necessitates examination of their cognitive, emotional, social, and creative lives. Through play, they are able to create new realities, gaining entrance into other dimensions outside the realm of adult scrutiny.

Access to high-quality care and educational programs outside the home is critical if children are to acquire the five developmental domains related to motor, literacy-numeracy (e.g., language and cognitive), social-emotional intelligence, and learning. It is essential that they have nurturing, attentive, and responsible adults and caregivers in their lives whose positive behaviors can be replicated as they assume more adultlike responsibilities. Their motivation to achieve and share their divine wisdom can precipitate a major shift in the way they reflect on the world around them.

Schools should be safe spaces where children's minds and souls are developed by teachers who instruct and mentally stimulate them with activities that tease out their innate intelligence. The feeling nature of children is growing and developing during "this heart of childhood." Soon they will be indoctrinated by societal beliefs and those of their families whose compassion and empathy, or lack thereof, will affect the trajectory their lives take well into the future.

Work the clay while it is still wet.

—Ethiopian proverb

A plethora of developmental milestones occur during adolescence. This life span (from age ten to twenty-one) is epic in its entirety. Adolescents grow in height and weight, pass from one grade to the next, start menstruating, experience their first wet dream, go to the prom, get a driver's license, graduate, receive their diplomas, secure their first job, and matriculate at a college. Their bodies are undergoing more developmental changes than at any other time except from birth to two years old. Their emotions are on a roller-coaster ride with mood swings that take them from sadness to anger to joy and back—from zero to sixty—in a matter of seconds. Their relationships with themselves and the entire world are a mass of confusion while life just keeps going around and around.

Parents, show you care and are aware. *Encourage* your sons and daughters to strive to become better and better versions of themselves. *Afford* them the compassion and empathy they need. *Support* them as they push through their fears. *Provide* positive feedback and discipline with an equal dose of rules and rewards. Be present as they articulate and process their feelings. *Aid* them as they quiet their minds and take the time to awaken, connect, and unify with their inner selves.

Anything that's mentioned can be managed. Share your own (uncensored) adolescent experiences and the challenges and adversity you faced *and* overcame. Make eye contact and be authentic, they need to know the real you. Whatever they see, they will eventually be. *Remind* them daily they are beloved children of the Most High God.

The curve of despondency starts at age eleven, peaks at age fifteen, and steadily declines until age twenty-three. So when negativity and heightened emotions emerge, let your child know it's time to put on the brakes, make a U-turn, and shift into the "yes" lane.

The rebellion, sensitivity to rudeness and humiliation, hierarchy of loves and loyalties, and the "I'm not a child, but I'm not quite an adult" and/or (s) are thought to be primitive artifacts that can be exhumed, examined, and left behind. But in fact, they are complex causal relationships that will be resurrected when biological processes that occurred during early infancy are reactivated during adolescence, initiated by complicated changes in the brain's neurochemistry.

In the words of G. Stanley Hall, "Adolescence is a new birth," a period of self-scrutiny, a deep dive into emotional terrain where conflicts once unveiled must be resolved so the higher and more completely human traits can be born.

The Second Quarter—Late Adolescence to Early Adulthood (Age 18–35)

> *Start where you are, with what you have. Make*
> *something of it and never be satisfied.*

—George Washington Carver,
botanist, inventor, professor at Tuskegee Institute

The developmental tasks that predominate in the two decades that encompass late adolescence to early adulthood center on the basic instinct to establish personal and economic independence, form intimate relationships with others, and explore identity. Cognition related to the practical aspects of life that permit judgment about important matters increases during this period. It is a time for realistic reflection as idealism decreases, a period in which emotions and subjective factors begin to influence intelligence.

> *I have a considerable amount of confidence but it's not in me.*
> *It's the work that God is doing in me that makes me confident.*

—Lauryn Hill, singer,
prolific songwriter, and rap artist

Eric Erikson describes early adulthood and its tentative uncertainty as a "moratorium—a period when a young person may not commit directly to life yet is working out the conditions inwardly that will make it possible to eventually do so."[1]

---

[1]   Thomas Armstrong, PhD, *The Human Odyssey: Navigating the Twelve Stages of Life* (Mineola, New York: Ixia Press, 2007), 133.

Early adulthood, with all its responsibilities and residual confusion, can create a cacophony of organized noise. Luckily, there are many ways to approach this new stage of growth once one declares, "This is my life. It's up to me to move in the direction that best suits my gifts and capabilities."

Put on your thinking cap. Work out a resolution between your own ideals and those of your parents and factor in your unique perception of what the world demands. Get serious about the rest of your life. In the end, it's all about the business of becoming your authentic self. The options you choose can set the tone for the life you live now and in the future.

The Third Quarter—Midlife (Age 36–52)

There is never time in the future in which we will work out our salvation. The challenge is in the moment; the time is always now.

—James Baldwin, author, activist

Midlife is a prime time to examine a broader landscape of one's life. It's a powerful, transformative period of adopting a more serious expression, taking life into one's full embrace and inviting dream-come-true experiences to manifest. However, there are two distinct sides to this coin. Midlife can also be a mirror reflection of the adolescent rites of passage, a hormone-charged emotional landmine where ruptures in identity and self-confidence can occur. It may feel like fifty has become the new fifteen.

You may be gripped by boredom, frustration, disappointment, and resentment, but don't despair. You're right where you should be, doing exactly what needs to get done. Take a respite from the competitive, dog-eat-dog mentality and reflect on the deeper meaning of this place in time, this great transition. Gaze inwardly and contemplate. Point your internal compass toward the source of your creative becoming. It is the hero's journey to retrieve one's deeper self, the better to advance and allow propulsion into the next phase. Refocus. Envision a rebirth of new probabilities for the years ahead.

The Fourth Quarter—Late Adulthood (Age 53–70)

We need in every community, a group of angelic troublemakers.

—Bayard Rustin, civil rights activist,
ideas architect/organizer of the March on Washington

Late adulthood represents the time of greatest life satisfaction complemented by the consciousness that "the best is (still) yet to come." Older adults have been gifted with the ability to nurture the mentor within and are equipped to care-give the future's progeny. Their emotional constancy gives them the balance to "stand between the generations" and take their rightful place as the anointed ones who preserve traditions and voice the cultural achievements that have stood the test of time.

Take the sting out of aging. Only VIPs make it this far. Set your attitude gauge on happy. Pursue regenerative interactions. Create giving relationships that can sustain you. Avoid all mental and emotional rigidity. Liberate yourself from any constraints placed on you. Dare to grow.

Snatch life up by the lapel and declare, "Baby, it's me and you." An extraordinary existence is well within your reach.

Overtime (70+)

The youth can walk faster, but it is the elder that knows the road.

—African Proverb

Among the Fon of Benin in West Africa, those in late adulthood are said to exist "between the two worlds of the living and the dead." An intersectionality that merges the ancient wisdom of the ancestors with the moral, aesthetic, and spiritual truths that are carried forward today.

You are our mothers, mentors, mature matriarchs, our father figures, furthering our futures, the keystone in our family structure possessing fidelity interwoven with the essence of honor.

You are our living angels, who, with eyes wide open, unveil the illusions and grasp the truer nature of things. You weather all the one-two punches and hard knocks life throws with supernatural grace. You neutralize acrimony and bitterness with fasting and prayer. You look up and aspire to the stars. As night follows day, you stand on the side of morality and righteousness placing the well-being of our own above your own.

You demonstrate an intense understanding of the dynamics of the human heart, a powerful knowing that is its own reward. You dreamed the world we are now living, bejeweled the crown, and placed it on our heads. We owe you our breath, our life, our love. You are the healing way.

In your reflection, aging serves as a form of ripening, a predetermined process that assumes a succulent, sweet, and savory taste. Take this time to luxuriate in that sweetness; stand in this unspeakable dawn.

LONGEVITY TO-DOS

Long life is in her right hand; in her
left hand are riches and honor.

—Proverbs 3:16 New International Version

The World Health Organization (WHO) defines health as "a dynamic state of complete physical, mental, spiritual, and social well-being," further stating that "the enjoyment of the highest attainable standard of health is one of the fundamental rights of every human being without distinction of race (ethnicity), religion, political belief, economic or social condition."

Living longer is not the key; staying healthy longer is. Do you want to be active and vital now and in your later years? Well, here are some longevity to-dos to get you started. Remember, the past cannot be changed, but the future is yet in your power.

Celebrate life.
Don't fixate on the calendar.
Every day is a gift.

Fast and pray.
Practice your faith. It can be your best medicine.

Meditate.
Quiet your mind. Release anxiety.
You're too blessed to be stressed.

Get plenty of sleep.
Nap regularly.
Cozy up to a better sex life and a brighter mood.

Be kind.
Surround yourself with pleasant people.
Treat others with love and care.

Expect respect.
Show others how to love you by always loving yourself.

Practice good self-care.
Maintain your self-esteem.
Stay engaged in productive and meaningful activities.
Extend random acts of kindness to others.

Develop stable relationships and social ties that bind.
It's a major boost for your health, and happiness especially for men.

Be conscientious.
Develop a strong work ethic. Continue to work as you grow older.
Hard work + prudence = an extended life span

Engage in regular exercise.
Work your mind *and* your body.
Stay in tip-top shape, inside and out.

Share your meals with family and friends.
Maintain a healthy microbiome. Feed the good bacteria in your gut.
Practice intermittent fasting.
Eat whole foods. Follow a primarily plant-based diet.
You are what you eat.

Stay hydrated.
Drink plenty of water. It's vital for joint and brain protection,
immune health, digestion, and balancing emotions.

Laugh.
It's a natural feel-good strategy that boosts the immune
system, relaxes muscles, aids circulation, and
protects against heart disease.

Make your own luck.
Be persistent and maintain a can-do attitude.
You alone are responsible for your happiness.

Keep a gratitude journal.
Thank-you is the highest prayer you can ever share.

Sources

Howard S. Friedman and Leslie R. Martin, *The Longevity Project: Surprising Discoveries for Health and Long Life from the Landmark Eight-Decades Study* (New York: Hudson Street Press, 2011).

Dan Buettner, *The Blue Zone Solutions—Lessons for Living Longer from the People Who've Lived the Longest,* National Geographic Books (Washington, DC, 2008).

GAME CHANGERS

For my people everywhere singing their slave
songs . . . For my people lending their strength to the
years . . . For my people standing staring trying to fashion
a better way . . . Let a new earth rise. Let another world
be born. Let a race of men now rise and take control.

—Margaret Walker,
excerpt from "For My People"
from *This Is My Century: New and Collected Poems*

My People / Myself

Live in truth. Offer words of good intent. Converse
with awareness. Speak positively of others. Follow
your inner guidance. Relate in peace. Act respectfully
of others. Advance through your own abilities.
Respect the property of others. Remain in balance
with your emotions. Achieve with integrity. Be open
to love in various forms. Benefit with gratitude. Be
a caretaker for the earth. Honor virtue. Embrace the
ALL. Affirm that all life is sacred. (Excerpt from the
42 Ideals of Ma'at)

It is not about supplication, it's about power. It's not about asking,
it's about demanding. It's not about convincing those who are
currently in power, it's about changing the very face of power itself.

—Kimberle Williams Crenshaw,
leading scholar of critical race theory and professor of law

I see protest as a genuine means of encouraging
someone to feel the inconsistencies, the horror of the
lives we are living. Social protest is saying that we

do not have to live this way. If we feel deeply and we encourage ourselves and others to feel deeply, we will find the germ of our answers to bring about change. Because once we recognize what it is we are feeling, once we recognize we can feel deeply, love deeply, can feel joy, then we will demand that all parts of our lives produce that kind of joy. And when they do not, we will ask, "Why don't they?" And it is the asking that will lead us inevitably toward change. (Audre Lorde; writer, poet, civil rights activist)

In all things that are purely social we can be as separate as the fingers, yet one as the hand in all things essential to mutual progress.

—Booker T. Washington, educator, author, presidential adviser, and leader of Tuskegee Normal and Industrial Institute (now Tuskegee University)

One Team / One Dream

Nurture collaborations that are deep and abiding. Establish purpose-driven partnerships. Familiarize yourself with truth-telling and reconciliation techniques. Maintain obedience to the Holy Spirit. Abide in awareness. Integrate your genius. Accelerate your thinking. Own your uniqueness. Reach higher, inspire, and acquire your utmost desires. Never give up, never give in. Be who God made you to be.

Charge them that are rich in this world . . . That they do good, that they be rich in good works, ready to distribute, willing to communicate; Laying up in store for themselves a good foundation against the time to come.

—1 Timothy 6:17–19 New International Version

The Makings of a Winner

1. Is bright, competitive, able to get along with others without conflict
2. Approaches situations with enthusiasm, maintains a dynamic attitude, jumps right in, and does whatever needs to be done
3. Persistent, faces failure as an inevitable step toward success
4. Finds the positive in the negative
5. Is appreciative of the things others do and shows gratitude for their efforts
6. Pays it forward by helping those in need
7. Determines that they will make a difference whenever and wherever possible
8. Stirs their internal fires and inspires others to feel good about doing the same

I decided that I would only do what reflected
positively on my father's life.

—Sidney Poitier, actor and author

Father Knows Best

1. Inspire and demonstrate a solid work ethic.
2. Push on despite setbacks, obstacles, and naysayers.
3. Serve as a supportive influence through life's ups and downs.
4. Give measured advice without suggesting what should be done.
5. Be present and nonjudgmental no matter the situation.
6. Strive to excel and thrive in the midst of success *and* failure.
7. When you fall, pick yourself up, then rise, and set even higher goals.
8. Make sound decisions, be dependable, and always look out for the best interests of others.
9. Do the right thing even when it's not popular.
10. Emphasize the importance of education.
11. Be a lifelong learner.
12. Develop the know-how to face challenges.

13. Make the seemingly impossible possible.

*My hope is that each of you will rise to the full height of your possibilities, which means the possession of these **eight cardinal virtues** which constitute a lady or a gentleman. May peace and prosperity be yours through life.*

—George Washington Carver

1. Be clean both inside and outside.
2. Neither look up to the rich or down on the poor.
3. Lose, if need be, without squealing.
4. Win without bragging.
5. Always be considerate of women, children, and older people.
6. Be too brave to lie.
7. Be too generous to cheat.
8. Take your share of the world and let others take theirs.

The Ten Basic "Stops . . ." Survivors of Racism Should Practice in Speech and/or Action

1. Stop Snitching
2. Stop Name-Calling
3. Stop Cursing
4. Stop Gossiping
5. Stop being Discourteous
6. Stop Stealing
7. Stop Robbing
8. Stop Fighting
9. Stop Killing
10. Stop Squabbling

—excerpt from *The United Independent Compensatory Code/System/Concept* by Neely Fuller Jr.

INTRODUCTION TO THE
FIRST QUARTER

Let the Games Begin

Imagine you are sitting front row center in a massive arena enmeshed in ambient light that exudes a calm, cool softness. This space in all its grandeur is reserved for champions. A sea of humanity is in the midst, with every ethnicity represented. Each is a recipient of a specially designed invitation, embossed with their name. You are a seed of that collective greatness, one of the chosen few, readying to be birthed into the world.

Before you came forth, you knew what would be expected of you. So your mental, physical, and spiritual self developed and evolved, attuned to meet the challenge. Be warned, once you arrive, you will be oblivious to the adventures to come.

It wasn't your intention to sit on the sidelines and be a spectator; you came to play. You have been assigned to a specific team and will be introduced to your predecessors, who walked the legacy to legend journey before you. At every given moment, the ball will be in your court and you alone can determine the game you want to play and its rules of engagement.

A succession of coaches, referees, and instructors will train you up in the way you should go, consistently reminding you of the inner strength and courage you possess. But there's no need to worry; you are the one running this race. This is the mind-over-matter journey of the champion.

You are focused on the spectacle before you as the roar of the crowd ignites in every language and dialect imaginable. Cheering, clapping, and foot stomping erupt in waves that reverberate. You gaze to the east, north, west, and south; in every direction there are legions, hundreds of thousands like you, who prepped for the competition with its requisite 274 days. Confident of your worthiness, you employ the patience needed as your arrival time nears.

The race will soon kick off, and you are at the starting line, crouched down in the start position, digits spread out and poised. Slowly inhaling and exhaling, you raise your head, looking to the right and left of you at your fellow contenders before centering your gaze front and center on what lies ahead.

Examining the scoreboard, tallying the winners and losers, the accumulation of runs, goals, touchdowns, dunk shots, and all the increments of time invested that will come later.

Now the focus must be on the engagement required to endure and successfully complete this arduous race. A single shot from the starter pistol ricochets, signaling that this momentous event has begun. On your mark, get set, go . . .

Let the games begin.

THE FIRST QUARTER

Conception to Early Adolescence (Age 0–17)

As of 2018, there are over seventy-three million children in the US.[1]

*What you decide on will be done; and light
will shine on your ways.*

—Job 22:28 New International Version

To win at the game of life you have to go all in. From the starter bell to the overtime, the finish line to the ultimate win has no shortcuts. You are your only limit, so go the distance.

You practiced, studied the plays, hit the game-winning shots, stood in the line of fire, took the blows, mopped up the mess, and found meaning in the message. No harm, no foul. It's only the first quarter, so you have a ways to go.

Trust and believe are a powerhouse, a quiet revolution. You stand on the shoulders of generations upon generations upon generations of melaninated achievers who ran and won their race.

Redeem the dream. Applaud your accomplishments. Broaden your vision. Be open to the hidden opportunities. Carve out a path toward renewed possibilities. And most importantly, never ever quit. Get out there and *win*. Let the roar of the crowd be heard.

---

[1]   US Census Bureau, Current Population Report, based on data derived from the national population projections released on December 2014.

Mothers weld immense power in the lives of their children, the "fruit of the womb, a gracious heritage from God."[2] It is in this inner earth, this succulent soil that babies-to-be grow, learn, and embody life's most profound lessons. A mother's job is to set her child up so that its souls can learn what is needed.

Motherhood as experienced and practiced in African diaspora culture is influenced by mythology and lore that speaks of the self-sacrifice, giving, and unconditional love associated with it. In many cultures, it is viewed as a sacred spiritual path, an exalted realm with imagery that idealizes the mother as creator, cradle rocker, nurturer, provider, and goddess. "She who knows the secrets of discovering heaven on earth."

The maternal symbolism of the supreme mother is seen in the Black Madonna (characterizing Christianity), Devi Ma (representing the Hindu tradition), Bodhisattva (the archetypal female), and the African creation goddess Mami Wata, who is associated with the moon and the ocean. While maternal archetypes far exceed paternal motifs, motherhood largely remains an unwritten story.

Black is the essence through which all color derives. Like the universe and the womb, African femininity is steeped in triple black/darkness and represents the original wo/man, the origin of all human life. Black women carry mitochondrial DNA (which is maternally inherited) that has all the variations possible for every different kind of human being on the earth. When the DNA of a black woman mutates, all other types of human beings come about. This is called the EVE gene (mtDNA).

Black women were considered the definition of beauty by all civilized nations so much so that the Greeks named the brightest constellation of stars after Queen Cassiopeia of Ethiopia (Aethiopia) and her daughter Andromeda. Writer and Afrocentric historian Dr. Yosef Ben-Jochannan once mused, "Dipped in chocolate, bronzed in elegance, enameled with grace, toasted with beauty, oh my lord, she's a black woman."

---

[2]   Ps. 127:3 KJV

*A father is neither an anchor to hold us back nor a sail to take
us there but a guiding light whose love shows us the way.*

—Anonymous

Fathers play an essential role in the developmental process of a new life. The Talmud states that when a father teaches his son, he teaches his son's son, thereby fostering a continuity and symmetry that spans across generations.

Fatherhood represents authority, guidance, leadership, and is a symbol of wisdom gained by age, experience, and self-contemplation. Ancient mythology denotes the virility, clarity, focus, power, dependability, and virtue associated with fathers.

A more comprehensive model defines fathers as "hu*man* beings who can readily access the masculine/feminine attribute suitable to effectively address each situation whether the desired outcome requires vulnerability, compassion, gratitude, mercy, or forgiveness, leaning toward self-care (and renewal) rather than self-sacrifice (and stress)."

The National Center for Health Statistics's 2013 survey found that black fathers are just as, and by many measures more, responsible caregivers than men of any other racial/ethnic group. Although the consistent refusal to acknowledge the hu*man*ity of black men can endanger them and undermine the mutually beneficial father-child relationships they seek.

A father's supportive presence is essential to the spiritual, psychological, and physical well-being of the family. Father presence is associated with gains in cognitive and language development, academic achievement, heightened empathy, self-esteem, and self-control, and is linked to a decrease in early puberty, depression, early sexual activity, and teen pregnancy in girls.

How do I put into words, those signals given me, some subtle, some not so subtle, that taught me, I am of a people?

—Phola Mabiezela, *The Way Things Were*

Black mothers and black fathers acknowledge the dignity, pride, and glory God and the ancestors poured to overflowing into your spirits, minds, and hearts. Reassert the intimate and intrinsic value of your families. Keep promises even when it hurts. Try harder than you ever thought possible to exemplify our story of radical radiance. Let your love and devotion be a nurturing and sustainable wellspring. Affirm the divine nature of our people. Restore your belief in one another; you are worthy and must now remember. Your children are individualized expressions of the Most High God. Raise them up in the ways they should go. They are ready for this world and came forth to be its liberators, empowered to secure and sustain our better tomorrows and brighter futures.

Black Parents-to-Be, Proceed with Caution

We are not the descendants of slaves, we are the descendants of prisoners-of-war.

—Dr. Edward Wesley Robinson, Jr., attorney, historian, author, and filmmaker

In his book *The Philadelphia Negro*, the first sociological case study of black Americans published in 1899, W. E. B. DuBois, PhD, conducted observations and research on the history and social status of forty thousand transplanted Africans residing in Philadelphia's Seventh Ward. The study pointed to the challenges imposed by racism and the lingering legacy of slavery, noting that the "high rates of black infantile mortality were a consequence of the poorer economic, social, and sanitary conditions black residents faced."[3]

---

[3]　W. E. B. DuBois, PhD, *The Philadelphia Negro: A Social Study* (New York: Benjamin Blom, 1899).

Black infants in the US are more than twice as likely to die as Caucasian infants—a racial disparity that is wider now than in 1850, fifteen years before the end of slavery, when the US first began recording infant mortality by ethnicity. Over four thousand black babies die each year, a morbidity attributable to racial inequities in the separate and unequal US health-care system.

Research shows that racially motivated differences in the quality of treatment at the site of care and delivery may contribute to the black-white disparity, a gap that accelerates as the mother's education and income rises. In fact, babies born to well-educated, middle-class and upper-class black mothers are "more likely to die by their first birthday than those born to Caucasian mothers with less than a high school education."[4]

According to recent research from the Center for Disease Control and Prevention (CDC), black women have the highest maternal mortality rate in the US and are nearly four times more likely to die than their Caucasian counterparts. Stress from racism is thought to be the primary culprit.

A black woman is 22 percent more likely to die from heart disease, 71 percent more likely to perish from cervical cancer, and 243 percent more likely to pass away from pregnancy- or childbirth-related complications. Blacks are disproportionately at risk due in part to substandard care from racially biased physicians and health-care practitioners.

Confronting Cumulative Wounds

The study of epigenetics has shown that human beings carry the physical attributes, emotional experiences, and transgenerational trauma of their parents, grandparents, and ancestors. For black women,

---

4   Laudan Y. Aron, "Despite Fifty Years of Improvements in Infant Mortality, Large Black-White Gap Remains Unchanged," *Urban Wire: Poverty, Vulnerability and the Safety Net* (blog), *Urban Institute,* August 25, 2013, https://www.urban. org/urban-wire/despite-fifty-years-improvements-infant-mortality-large-black-white-gap-remains-unchanged.

this is a particularly problematic conundrum, given the denial of their human right to maintain body, sexual, and reproductive autonomies and to bear, nurture, and parent their own children in supportive and sustainable communities without government interference and the systemic oppression that undergirds it.

This violation of *reproductive justice*, a term coined by a group of black women in 1994, can be traced back to 1845 when Dr. James Marion Sims, the infamous father of modern gynecology, used enslaved black girls and women who had endured sexual and reproductive violence on the plantation as guinea pigs in experimental (and excruciatingly painful) operations conducted in his backyard without anesthesia or sanitary safeguards. Sims built his reputation among wealthy plantation owners by treating their "human property." It was sexual assault masked as research that represents medical apartheid's long, ethically bereft history.

"In the South," Harriet A. Washington writes in her book *Medical Apartheid: The Dark History of Medical Experimentation on Black Americans from Colonial Times to the Present*, "rendering black women infertile without their knowledge during other surgery was so common that the procedure was called a Mississippi Appendectomy." This abhorrent history of systematic sexual and reproductive malfeasance illuminates the dehumanization and attempted genocide of the black body, more than justifying the distrust of the "health-care" system that continues to perpetuate it. However, Washington maintains (and rightly so) that "African Americans desperately need the medical advantages and revelations that only ethical, essentially therapeutic research initiatives can give them."

> *That strong mother doesn't tell her cub, 'Son,*
> *stay weak so the wolves can get you.' She says,*
> *'Toughen up, this is reality we are living in.'*

> —Lauryn Hill

Eugenics was the neologism coined by Sir Francis Galton in 1883 to define the improvement of the inborn quality of humankind by better breeding. The eugenics movement had a significant political appeal between 1900 and 1945, attracting advocates from across the political spectrum. Eugenics policies were implemented through sterilization laws in both the US and Europe and lasted until the 1970s, when the civil rights movement undermined its legitimacy. The rise of eugenics was strictly connected to important scientific developments, particularly in the emergence of genetics and the modern view of biological heredity. After 1945, arguments about racial or innate inequalities were increasingly treated with suspicion and, unofficially, marginalized. The legacy of eugenics remains a debated topic with the mapping of the human genome that shapes the postgenomic landscape.

The Eugenics Board of North Carolina's government-run, federally funded program, referred to as North Carolina's Holocaust, coerced the sterilization of nearly eight thousand preteens, teens, and adults between 1929 and 1976. Nationwide, over sixty thousand blacks, Native Americans, and Latin men, women, and children were targeted, a history that is deeply rooted in white feminism and its shame-faced, bed-partner racism and white supremacy. African Americans must ensure, by any means necessary, that our God-given right to bear children overcomes any societal objectives that would serve to circumscribe it.

Heal Thy Self

All trauma, stress, and loss impact women's biology in the womb and subtly alter the symmetry of the spiritual, mental, and physical bodies. Those memories reverberate throughout the body recording and responding to emotional triggers in a language that can be translated and communicated. Our thoughts and emotions affect the heart's magnetic field, which modifies the energetic frequency levels of those in our environment. In both literal and metaphorical senses, the body keeps the score.

Stress ignites uncertainty, which leads to anxiety and feelings of vulnerability. Be aware when these emotions surface. Ask yourself, "What is being experienced here?" Everything that is said repeatedly out loud or in our thoughts is an affirmation that must, by universal law, manifest. The reticular activating system (RAS) is an aspect of our brain that makes words that get repeated over time part of our identity. Our thoughts and beliefs influence the quantum reality, which is the source of the material world.

Nourish and affirm positive thoughts, feelings, and actions repeatedly. Lovingly proclaim, "I am protected. It's safe to go inside." Journey into the inner reaches of your being with compassion and gentle kindness. You are so much more than you think you are and infinitely more than you have been lead to believe.[5]

Neurofeedback, meditation, mindfulness, yoga, drama, and sports offer a road to recovery from trauma by activating the brain's natural neuroplasticity. Befriend your body, own it and the physical experiences you've had. Rely on the mastery of your body, the safety of your body, the capacity to find peace within your body.

Life Gives a Lot for All It Takes

> *They will not labor in vain, nor will they bear children*
> *doomed to misfortune; for they will be a people blessed*
> *by the Lord, they and their descendants with them.*

—Isaiah 65:23 New International Version

With conscious conception, the welcoming of a soul is a reverent act, a communal undertaking with the expectant father, siblings, family,

---

[5]   Deepak Chopra, *How to Know God: The Soul's Journey Into the Mystery of Mysteries* (New York: Harmony Books, 2000) 222.

and other loved ones—the "womb village"—tasked to create a safe and sacred space where the child's ever-evolving potential can be nurtured.[6]

For that to occur, all mental, emotional, spiritual, and ancestral patterning (experienced by both expectant parents) must be openly and honestly dealt with. Before making the decision to have a baby, examine the state of your physical body and investigate any illnesses you have experienced, challenges you have endured, anxieties you carry, any mental illnesses or depression you or your family have had, any unresolved bereavement, grief, and loss, and most importantly, the beliefs you hold about your body and your relationship with it. Gain awareness of how you handle stress, fear, vulnerability, and the prospect of death.

Be cognizant that your birth narrative—from spiritual, psychological, and physiological perspective—can play an integral role in your ability or inability to conceive.

Bon Voyage—Your Conscious Conception Journey Is Setting Sail

Parents-to-be, plan to begin your conscious conception journey at least six to nine months before you conceive. Release and embody love from within. Listen deeply and be obedient to your inner spirit. Make intentional choices and take compassionate action. Nurture and preserve loving and harmonious relationships. Transfer pure and positive vibrations to the womb. Make an authentic soul connection with your baby through prayer, meditation, and visualization.

Unleash the latent power of your mind and the potency of high-frequency thoughts, emotions, and imagination will be activated. Embark on this journey fully vetted, check the root causes of all stress and trauma, undergo a thorough detox and acquire the emotional readiness needed, and the joy of parenthood can be yours. It's your

---

6   "Conscious Conception for a Healthy Pregnancy and Happy Babies," *The Times of Africa*, October 12, 2016.

charge to give birth to a healthy, stress-free, and trauma-free being whose day-to-day present *and* future will be a privilege to live.

The Power of Conscious Breathing

Conscious breathing is one of many methods used to clear trauma from the body. Pranayama (the extension of breath) invokes states of deep releasing, calling in the unfolding-into-consciousness we pray for when feelings of separation arise. Breathe all the things you've refused to speak. Allow yourself to intentionally feel all the better-left-unspoken experiences rising with each inhalation.

Connecting past emotion with physical intention is akin to having a surgical procedure that sutures the wounds that have been left open. Energetically, the space in the lower abdomen (the solar plexus chakra) is where insecure thoughts and old traumas congregate, which often surfaces and resurfaces over time. When you resist, whatever you are pushing against persists then expands and grows larger.

Another Healing Modality

To further support optimal fertility (as well as digestive and emotional health), consider incorporating Mayan Abdominal Therapy into your "heal thy self" regime. This protocol is an external, noninvasive abdominal manipulation (suitable for both genders) that repositions internal organs that have shifted, thereby disrupting the flow of blood, lymph, nerve connections, and chi (life force energy).

By moving the uterus back into place, the natural balance of the body is restored in the pelvic area and in the surrounding organs. Fibroid tumors, endometriosis, and cesarean deliveries are decreased when uterine massage is utilized.

For men, Mayan Abdominal Therapy unblocks energy channels, alleviating swelling, inflammation, premature ejaculation, frequent urination, and problems with impotency by sending a full blood supply to the prostate. The abdomen is the power center, the seat of strength (pain, grief) and transformation. Our "will" is located in our subtle body at the level of the navel. When we communicate through that center, we're empowered to interpret and implement its unique curative linguistics.

Conception

We are born of love; Love is our mother.

—Rumi, thirteenth-century
Persian poet and Sufi mystic

Like every idea that's initiated and grown within the heart, a baby is first a thought thought upon long enough to become a reality. You can't see the baby, smell it, taste it, or touch it. The baby is but a dream, a desire until it is birthed into the world. The virtue this life span embodies is *hope*.

When a child is conceived, a wide range of emotions erupt within the mother *and* father—fear, joy, uncertainty, love. This rambunctious bundle of joy has carved a path that his or her parents must now take care in the twinkle of an eye, forging a divine purpose that was cut from distant stars. What the baby is to be, it is now becoming.

Consider broadening mommy-to-be's birth-to-postpartum journey by incorporating the loving presence of a doula, a birthing companion or coach who administers one-on-one client care and emotional support, which can reduce mortality rates, the risk of cesarean sections, lower the need for medical intervention, shorten labor time, and improve birth outcomes. It is a plus for black women who deserve compassionate birthing partnerships and birth experiences that affirm and honor their reproductive and human rights.

Floyd L. Griffin Jr.

I prayed for this child, and the Lord has
granted me what I asked of him.

—1 Samuel 1:27 New International Version

The very earliest beginnings from conception to birth influence a multitude of intrinsic genetic and environmental factors that affect physiological and psychological development throughout the life span. Social, emotional, cognitive, perceptual, and moral development are not confined to specific life quarters. They are specifically expressed in each of the life cycles.

After conception, when the sperm and ovum fuse, a process of cleansing is initiated where most chemical marks on the genes are stripped away. As the egg grows and develops, genetic reshuffling occurs as cells differentiate into their specific functions.

From zygote to birth, human development progresses in an orderly sequence and speeds up during the prenatal stage. At approximately fourteen days, the zygote turns into an embryo and at nine weeks a fetus, over one hundred times greater than the zygote in size. The period of greatest physical growth is when the beginnings of a brain, kidneys, liver, and the digestive tract are forming before birth.

At three months, the embryo's brain impulses coordinate the function of its organ systems so that the fetus may now swallow amniotic fluid in and out of the lungs and occasionally urinate. Its internal reproductive organs have primitive eggs or sperm cells. If stroked, the embryo reacts by flexing its trunk, extending its head, and moving its arms in a backward motion.

The fetus does not breathe in the womb. The mother breathes for it, dispensing essential oxygen passed through the umbilical cord. The fetus does, however, make breathing-like movements beginning at nine weeks of pregnancy so it can replicate that movement after birth.

The mother may start to feel the fetus kicking, a movement known as quickening, which many consider the beginning of human life. The reflex activities of the wands and bulbs of shadowy light that are the toes and heels become brisker as muscular development increases.

At five months, the fetus is showing distinct personality traits with preferred positions in the uterus and defined wake-sleep patterns. This is a time when the fetal heartbeat can be distinctively heard. At seven months, the fetus has fully formed features and can cry and suck its thumb. The hidden structure of the fetal body is a beautiful and perfect mirror of the world it will soon enter. Approximately a week before birth, the fetus stops growing as it is fast surpassing the perimeters of its living environment. The organ system is operating efficiently, and the heart rate is increasing, readying the baby for the transition of life outside the womb.

It is quite an ordeal as the baby dives head first, spending hours squeezing through the narrow walls of the birth canal. The struggle to emerge from the dark warmth of the womb may be Mother Nature's way of aiding in this sacred transition.

Be mindful that the umbilical cord should never be cut and clamped. Cord circulation should be allowed to continue for thirty-plus minutes after birth, so there won't be an immediate need for the baby to use its lungs. The oxygen from the cord allows the stem cells, blood, and vital nutrients to continue pumping into the baby, letting the cord detach on its own allows for maximum stem cell and blood transfusion resulting in a healthier, more highly developed newborn.

The Importance of Touch

> *Touch is a child's first language. Understanding spoken language comes long after understanding touch.*

—Dr. Frederick Leboyer,
French physician and natural childbirth advocate

During pregnancy, a baby is as close as can be to his or her mommy, getting warmth, nutrition, protection, and oxygen directly from her body. Labor and birth disrupts the baby's access to the security of the womb, although a subtle rebalancing can occur when skin-to-skin, or kangaroo care, is applied for one to two hours after birth.

Place the newborn on his or her mother's bare chest, between her breasts, draping a blanket over both of them for warmth and comfort. If the mother is unable to provide kangaroo care, then the father can gladly step in. Encourage the dad to set aside an hour or two of skin-to-skin cuddle time with his little precious one, and he will experience the depths of love that can be transferred through tender touch.

The benefits are evident within the first few minutes as the baby's body temperature, blood sugar levels, breathing, and heart rates stabilize as good bacteria is being transferred. Skin-to-skin care boosts maternal-child bonding, offering an easy transition from the womb. It enhances parent-baby communication, relieves pain, reduces crying, and assists in initiating breastfeeding.

According to UNICEF, "Every newborn, when placed on the mother's abdomen, soon after birth, has the ability to find its mother's breast all on its own and to decide when to take the first breastfeed, which is referred to as the breast crawl."

Breastfeeding is a natural way to save babies' lives, reduce rates of malnutrition, support children's health, and is associated with improved performance in intelligence tests and increased educational attainment, productivity, and income in adulthood. Numerous studies confirm that neonatal mortality can be reduced by 22 percent when breastfeeding is initiated by the mother within one hour of birth.

Other forms of touch therapy, like infant massage, can be equally beneficial. Infant massage is an ancient practice used primarily in cultures where touch is thought to inspire both physical and spiritual well-being. Maoris, the indigenous Polynesian people of New Zealand, incorporate infant massage into regular bath time to improve a child's gracefulness and suppleness.

Infant massage can activate certain physiological changes associated with growth and development positively affecting the infant hormones that control stress, strengthening the immune system, regulating digestive, respiratory, and circulatory systems, congestion, and teething with special strokes used to relieve discomfort from gas and colic. Studies suggest that when applied with moderate pressure, massage can promote growth for premature babies and those with asthma, diabetes, and certain skin disorders.

Massage is mutually beneficial, helping parents understand and respond to their baby's nonverbal cues while promoting confidence and competence in their caregiving abilities. Cross-cultural research shows that babies who are breastfed, massaged, carried, rocked, and lovingly held demonstrate a greater degree of compassion and cooperation in later life spans.

Incorporate massage into your baby's normal routine. Plan your bonding and relaxation time at least one hour after feeding. Create a warm and soothing environment, with soft lighting or nontoxic candles. Before you begin, place the baby on a thick plush towel, make eye-to-eye contact, smile, and send loving and healing vibrations to him or her from toe to head.

Indian milking is a gentle stroking of the legs while the twist and squeeze is a light compression of the muscles in the thigh and calf. Apply the strokes with utmost delicacy, taking into account your little one's fragility.

To familiarize yourself with the proper techniques and/or identify certified instructors in your area, contact the International Association of Infant Massage (IAIM).

You *need 4 hugs a day for survival, 8 hugs a day for maintenance, and 12 hugs a day for health.*

—Virginia Satir, psychotherapist and family therapist

Studies have shown that children who are deprived of hugs during infancy may experience difficulty showing and sharing love. Hugs are natural painkillers that boost the immune system, releasing endorphins into the body that create a sense of euphoria. Hugging allows you to make and fulfill a vital human connection and be a recipient of the most affirming and powerful form of nonverbal communication. By sharing a hug or embrace, you are expressing the high frequency of love through your heart chakra (*Anahata*), the center through which all virtuous emotions emanate.

We are cut from the same cloth of humanity, bound by a shared commitment to exist in love, "the threshold of another universe." Spirituality is the bridge across which we access the divine, that all-encompassing higher power that is our source and our sustenance.

Empirical evidence shows that spirituality is an inborn aspect of our heredity as fundamental to our makeup as our emotions and physical senses are. Natural spirituality links the trinity of brain, mind, and body, allowing us to be in alignment with aspects of ourselves that are eternal. Spirituality lingers at the entrance to our inner universe, reminding us in the present that "our futures are more beautiful than all our pasts."

Parents play an integral role in the development of their child's spirituality, which is a vital biological and psychological imperative; its attunement begins whole and is fully expressed at birth. A child's spirituality thrives in the light of parental attention and support. When children believe there's a higher power that watches over them, it creates a deeper sense of well-being, planting seeds of lasting happiness and lifelong thriving.

Young children are versed in the language of spirit and fluent in its ancient, timeless, nonverbal dimensions. Evidence of which is poignantly expressed in the story of orator, public servant, and ordained elder Joshua Kenyatta Mack:

> A son of promise, integrity, dignity and divine love, offering agency to the goodness of all.

> "I first saw the hand of God when I was six, sitting on the linoleum bathroom floor with my mom. She had a lot of health issues and was dealing with kidney stones, problems with her lungs, which required the use of an oxygen tank, and menstrual cramps. While we were sitting there together, she asked me to pray for her.

> At that time, I didn't know anything about God or even have any concept of church. But I pushed on. I said, 'God, my mom believes in you,' and miraculously he healed her. I saw the lumps in her belly go away. I remember a series of things had happened that day with God supernaturally coming to the scene.

> What that situation did for me was show me that God could intervene. I didn't like the fact that he could intervene but didn't and that the world was separated from him. How do I mesh those worlds that seem separate but are in fact One?

> Any parent who hopes better for their children should strengthen their own relationship with God. My mom was influential in my walk with Christ, it was her humility that made all the difference.

Young children are blessed with spiritual qualities that are inherent— their open curiosity, compassion, and loving ways and how they instinctively respond from the heart. If supported in childhood, spirituality can become a significant resource for health and healing throughout adulthood and serve as an internally based support system that offers meaningful genetic contributions.

All of nature speaks to and through the *how* and *what* of spirituality, engaging us through a smile, a newborn baby, a rainbow, the flutters of a butterfly's wings, or a loving heart. Parents can strengthen the spiritual connection and extend the field of family love through imaginative, interactive engagement.

Ask your child to draw his or her own field of love. Encourage him or her to think about the spiritual presence that resides in the field. Let him or her see and know for himself or herself that the field of love is there in good *and* bad times and can be a source of deep healing. Look at the drawing often, and imagine God's hand expanding the family's field of love.

When families employ and maintain spiritual or contemplative practice, synchronization of regions of the brain occurs, facilitating mental, physical, and soul elevation.

Infancy and Childhood

Infancy and childhood span from birth to the adolescent years during which the individual grows physically, cognitively, and socially. Infants' psychological development relies on their biological development. To understand the emergence of motor skills and memory, you must understand the developing brain.

Infants are born with certain innate abilities. Early on, they show a sophisticated social and emotional awareness that is a key part of child development. At forty-two minutes old, newborns can imitate facial expressions, and at one month old, they can stick out their tongue when they see someone else do it. At five months old, infants possess numerical concepts suggesting that humans are innately endowed with arithmetical abilities, according to research by psychologist Karen Wynn. At nine months old, infants can associate happy facial expressions with a happy tone of voice (showing surprise when an expression and tone of the voice don't match).

"Children are active thinkers, constantly trying to construct more advanced understandings of the world," child psychologist Jean Piaget wrote. "It is with children that we have the best chance of studying the development of knowledge." Cognitive development is indicative of changes in thought processes that result in a growing ability to acquire and utilize knowledge. Research related to cognitive development in newborns found that infants pay more attention to new objects than ones they are familiar with, which translates into learning.

Piaget believed that the driving force behind intellectual development is the biological development that occurs in conjunction with our experiences and the schemas or mental molds into which we store them. Cognitive development is shaped by the errors we make.

The process of assimilation involves incorporating new experiences into our current understanding (schema), a process of adjustment and modification that is referred to as accommodation.

Piaget's stages of cognitive development begin at the sensorimotor stage (birth to two) when infants experience the world through their senses (looking, hearing, touching, mouthing) and action (grasping) with stranger anxiety developing at around eight months. While Piaget's theories have influenced ideas related to growth and development in many cultures globally, contemporary researchers refute his theory that children in this developmental stage lack the capacity to think. Believing instead that development is a continuous process with children expressing their mental ability at an earlier age and that formal logic is a smaller part of cognition. In addition to counting and understanding abstract concepts and ideas, young children can even comprehend the basic laws of physics.

The development of the brain unfolds based on genetic instructions, causing various bodily and mental functions to occur in sequence—standing before walking, babbling before talking—which is referred to as maturation. Maturation sets the basic course of development, while experience modifies it.

Maturation and motor development is first seen when infants begin to roll over, sit unsupported (at six months), crawl (at eight to nine months), begin to walk (at twelve months), and walk independently (at fifteen months). Experience affects the timing in which this sequence occurs. According to Erikson's theory of psychosocial development, the key question to be explored and answered is "Is my world safe?" The virtue associated with this life span is *hope*.

Attachment

Bodily contact and familiarity lead to attachment, which is secured when a baby bestows a sense of trust upon a parent or primary caregiver. For positive childhood attachment patterns to develop, parents must be warm, attentive, and responsive toward their little ones. In cultures where mothers and fathers share child-rearing responsibility, similar secure attachments such as social and emotional competency and literacy develop.

Most children are able to explore their environments in the presence of their mother, father, guardian, or caregiver without experiencing distress when that person departs—out of sight, out of mind. However, separation anxiety peaks at thirteen months regardless of whether the child is in or outside the home.

Parental support must never be withheld for an extended period of time. Otherwise the child is at risk of experiencing the physical, psychological, and/or social difficulties that can alter the levels of the brain's serotonin, the neurotransmitter important in the inhibition of anger and aggression.

Conscious Parenting

The one's that matter most are the children.

—Lakota proverb

In the succeeding stanzas, Kahlil Gibran captured the very essence of conscious parenting in his melodic meditations on the divine nature of children, which were soulfully crafted in his book, *The Prophet*:

Your children are not your children
They are the sons and daughters of
Life's longing for itself

The connective tissue of those who came before and those who are yet to be, a fragile process that children maintain awareness of throughout early childhood. Young children are self-empowered to express their soul connection to God. The temples they are born into are crowns of creation, divined natural arrangements that hold the hopes, dreams, and the mansions of possibility yet to be demonstrated. Children are designed for optimal expenditures of energy and possess the stamina and spiritual acuity to thrive.

When parents speak of their children, a deep intimacy emerges and acts of expansive love stretch forth like the ebbing tide. It's the christening of a lifelong journey.

They come through you but not from you,
and though they are with you, yet they belong not to you.
You may give them your love but not your thoughts.
For they have their own thoughts.

As conscious parents, you have continually developed and nurtured your higher self; now is the appointed time to assist your child in that sacred process. Support your child's emotional intelligence—their capacity to be aware of, control, and express emotions—and handle interpersonal relationships with wisdom and empathy. Teach them how to recognize their feelings and understand the origin of those feelings and how to effectively deal with them so they do not later manifest as trauma or pain. Allow your child the space and energy to navigate their inner geography. Developing the embodiment of your child's truest self through authentic exploration represents conscious parenting at its best.

When you guide your little one's journey into their inner being-ness, they will begin expressing a version of who they really are. Tap into their heightened intelligence, and over time, their ability to align with their best selves will naturally occur. Children are intrinsically empowered to maneuver through life on their own terms, owning every aspect of life and the process through which those cumulative experiences came forth.

Look them in the eye and let them know they are perfect, whole, and complete. Recognize what an honor and privilege it is to be present as they envision themselves as divine expressions of the Most High God.

Support them in answering the difficult questions:

- Who am I? (identity based on the physical environment and the body)
- What do I desire for myself? (awareness based on independent decision-making)
- What are my goals, and how will I achieve them? (knowledge based on survival or self-realization)

You've already undergone this internal inquiry, and therefore, you are confident that your child can develop a relationship with their own success, see its value and the effort it may require. This is a process they should be able to comprehend by age six or seven.

There are things they will need to do to get the desired result. Let them know you'll be there to help. When you plant those auspicious seeds (of thought), you are building a foundation they can be rooted in.

Feed your children pure, clean foods that provide the nutrients needed for their growth, development, and optimal health. Engage them in physical activity to maintain a healthy weight, improve self-confidence, and support positive mental health. Create a safe and sacred place where they can honor their own lives, showing up and showing out for themselves.

At times, you may find it difficult to acknowledge this as a holy moment-to-moment collaboration. When that occurs, put your know-it-all ego on pause (so it won't rear its ugly head) and exit the fear-based survival mode. Honor your own definition of what constitutes worthiness. Delete any feelings of blame, shame, and/or guilt that may arise. Renew your mind, and renew your life with discernment, discipline, and the utmost care. Forgive your own parents; they did the very best they knew how to do. You may struggle, but with consistency, a gradual unfolding will occur. Remember, you (and your child) are rising to a higher vibration together. *You are the bow. Your child is the living arrow that is being sent forth.*

The Preschool Years—Age 3–5

Preschoolers are inquisitive, independent, imaginative, and enthusiastic, and they are capable of successfully navigating the ever-evolving world in which they live. They are eager learners who need to touch, taste, smell, hear, and test things, stimulating their human senses as they gain knowledge through experience, participation, and play.

Piaget believed that children in the preoperational stage (age two to seven) use intuitive reasoning to associate words with things and images that exist in their environment. They walk (then run) on tiptoes, balance (then hop) on one foot, jump horizontally, skip, dance, climb, and roll—an active and aggressive full-body biological process that integrates the logical and creative parts of the brain.

Preschoolers enjoy strengthening their manual dexterity by unzipping, unsnapping, and unbuttoning their clothes, lacing and tying their shoes, handling small objects, throwing a ball overhead, cutting on a line with scissors, and drawing in circular and horizontal motions.

The virtues associated with the early childhood-preschool stages are *will* and *purpose*, the sense of personal control and independence that manifests when the following questions, Can I do things by myself? Am I good or bad? are affirmatively answered.

In order to develop socially and emotionally, preschoolers need clear and concise rules and must be consistently reminded of the consequences associated with certain behavior. Encourage them to express their feelings verbally. Praise them for their achievements. Be affectionate and compassionate. They need to feel important and worthwhile. Catch them doing something good. Create opportunities to affirm to them that they are loved. Investing your time and effort will help them better understand their mental state and that of others.

Preschoolers can also be bossy—bragging busybodies who are talkative, rowdy, and obnoxious, singing, rhyming, making up words, and asking lots and lots of questions that can stimulate the (surprisingly) serious conversations they crave. They find freedom and independence by communicating their needs, ideas, and asking those pesky nonstop questions, all of which supports intellectual development.

At five years old, they enter the "look at me" phase, hopping, doing somersaults, walking forward and backward, kicking balls, climbing, swinging, and other attention-getting movement milestones they will master in the coming year.

Peekaboo, Peekaboo: The Power of Play

Play is essential to the acquisition of social and motor skills as well as cognitive thinking, which is crucial throughout the life spans. At an early age, play allows children to utilize their creativity, develop their imagination, dexterity, and physical and emotional strength, providing the opportunity to engage and interact with their surroundings and with their parents as they help them master the world around them. G. Stanley Hall asserted that play builds character, discipline, obedience, and moral strength.

Play can also be used as a tool to develop creative behavior that inspires divergent thinking, expanding thought in different directions and connecting that which was previously never connected but is functioning as yet unseen. There are six stages associated with Mildred Parten Newhall's theories as it relates to preschooler's participation in play, noted as follows:

- Unoccupied play—when a baby performs random movements or is just observing.
- Solitary (or independent) play—when a child maintains focus on an activity, unaware or uninterested in what others are doing, which is most common in ages two to three.
- Onlooker play (behavior)—when the child watches others (but does not participate) engaging in conversations about the play and other social interactions.
- Parallel play (adjacent play, social coaction)—when the child plays separate but adjacent to others, close enough to mimic their actions.

- Associative play—when the child is interested in the people playing but not in coordinating their activities.
- Cooperative play—when there is interest in both the people playing and the activity being played, which is organized with participants being assigned or given designated roles. This stage of play requires advanced social maturity and organizational skills rarely seen in preschool. Human developmentalists question whether there is a sequence associated with these stages of play.

Culturally relevant play is represented in noncompetitive hand-clapping games typically played by two as a rhythmic accompaniment to songs from black musical traditions, like "Shake It To the One that You Love the Best," "Uno, Dos Sierra," "Down Down Baby," and a host of others—all of which improve hand-eye coordination and finger or hand dexterity.

Double Dutch is a culturally relevant jump rope game (involving two turners with separate ropes) played primarily by girls as they chant rhymes, hop on one foot, bounce a ball, pick up and put down objects in between jumping, and/or adding styles and tricks such as pop-ups, mambos, and around the world.

It is an aerobic workout that can incorporate a mash-up of squats, jumping jacks, push-ups, and other arm exercises. Jump high and listen to the rhythm. Double Dutch can be traced back to AD 1600 when the Egyptians used vines for jumping.

Reading Is FUNdamental

> *Reading is dreaming with open eyes.*
>
> —Anissa Trisdianty

Nurture a love for language and literacy by reading to your baby in utero, creating soothing, rhythmic, and familiar sounds s/he can hear by week 25. Research suggests that babies can understand language patterns and, after birth, recognize words they first heard in the womb. Reading kick-starts brain development, early language learning, and prereading skills, stimulating lifelong cognition across the life span. It also improves the quality of parent-infant relationships through increased cuddle time, reciprocal eye-to-eye contact, talking to one another, and facial expressions/gestures exchanged between Mommy and Daddy and the little one(s).

To optimize the shared book reading experience for your infant, choose books with faces or objects that are individually named, which can help them learn more and apply what they've learned to new experiences. The benefits will extend from the first year of life to four years into childhood. Pick out culturally responsive, age-appropriate books that affirm their intelligence and unique cultural heritage with characters that look like them sharing stories that reflect their personal interests. Choose picture books, pop-ups, repetitive nursery rhythms, classic fairy tales, or biographies they can read alone or enjoy with Mom, Dad, or an older sibling. Make reading a fun, focused family tradition. Get a library card for your kindergartner. Encourage them to check out books and attend story-time programs and other literary events together.

Create a reading nook for your little ones with a child-sized table, chairs, and a bookcase they can easily access. As your child gets older, introduce books that teach tolerance, mindfulness, emotional intelligence, and the history of the African diaspora culture, and its melanated icons. Celebrate authors like Vashti Harrison, Jabari Asim, Andrea Davis Pinkney and poets Nikki Grimes and Lucille Clifton, beloved wordsmiths who creatively capture(d) worlds inhabited by "all us who came cross the water."

School Days

School-age development can be described as the physical, emotional, and mental abilities associated with children ages six to eleven. At ages five, six, and seven, children exhibit a tremendous amount of excitement as it relates to school and the soon-to-come experiences that are on the horizon.

While six- and seven-year-olds may progress at differing rates and possess diverse interests, most have reached certain milestones as it relates to motor development (well-developed hand-eye coordination and good balance), language and thinking development (several thousand word vocabulary, longer attention span, thoughtful and reflective thinking, the ability to tell time, distinguish between daytime and nighttime, and solve more complex problems), and social and emotional development (strong emotional reactions, the desire to be perfect, and the ability to differentiate between right and wrong).

The quest to assume more adultlike responsibility emerges in middle childhood (ages nine to eleven) as the way they view themselves and reflect on their world shifts, amplifying the need to have adults in their midst who embody wholesome behavior and a positive mental outlook. Eight- and nine-year-olds groom and dress themselves independently, count backward, understand fractions and concepts of space, and take more pleasure in reading. Ten- to twelve-year-olds can craft stories that inspire enlightenment and write letters that engage the imagination while relishing the opportunity to communicate with friends and family. Piaget's concrete operational stage theorizes that given the proper materials, a child in that life span should be equipped to think logically about outcomes, perform mathematical functions, and mentally grasp factual analogies.

Importance is placed on being industrious, adapting to the surrounding world, and grasping the coping mechanisms necessary to meet new social and academic demands. Parental attention, encouragement, and support are the keys to success both inside and outside the classroom.

The virtue associated with this life stage is *competence*, the ability to acquire a sense of confidence and worthiness, emphasizing, "Yes, I know I can do good."

Piaget's formal operational stage can occur as early as age seven, although he theorized it begins at age twelve when the ability to think abstractly, reason hypothetically, and engage in scientific intellection occurs.

Phillis Wheatley's ability to assimilate, accommodate, and find balance in her new reality epitomizes Piaget's theory. Transported as human cargo on a ship that bore her name, this daughter of Africa arrived in Boston at the age of eight with her genius fully intact. She possessed an inner and outer life that, despite societal convention, was sacred, holy, and worthy of veneration.

She was met not only with acceptance but adoration for her countenance, poise, and prose. Many would prostrate at the altar of her words, one alphabet after another, forming her first body of work at age twelve with a compilation of soulful psalms published eight years later in 1773.

Below is an example of Phillis Wheatley's poem:

A R I S E, my soul, on wings enraptur'd, rise
To praise the monarch of the earth and skies, Whose goodness and beneficence appear
As round its centre moves the rolling year,

Or when the morning glows with rosy charms, Or the sun slumbers in the ocean's arms:Of light divine be a rich portion lent
To guide my soul, and favour my intent. What
songs will arise, so constant, so divine.

Throughout history, black girl magic has been unstoppable, a force of nature with the intuitive, intellectual, and imaginative power of girls like Wheatley in full effect, as witnessed in the activism of Naomi

Wadler and the entrepreneurial spirit of Mikaila Ulmer, both eleven years old, the business acumen of thirteen-year-old Asia Newsome, the comic book series written by nine-year-old Natalie McGriff, and the sustainable/wearable art by sixteen-year-old fashionista and illustrator Maya Penn.

Journeying Toward Adolescence

Puberty ushers in a period of human development during which physical growth and sexual maturity occur, characterized by intense hormonal shifts that signal in boys the onset of semenarche (first ejaculation) and breast development in girls with menarche (first menstruation) occurring approximately two years after. This developmental process is related to adrenarche, the maturation of the cortex of the adrenal glands, the two triangle-shaped endocrine organs that sit above the kidney.

Puberty occurs in girls anywhere from age six to eleven and in boys from age nine to twelve, leaving them (as tweens) stuck smack dab in the middle—too old to be children but too young to be teens. The most evident signs of puberty in boys are pubic hair (purbarche), enlargement of the testicles, and adultlike body odor caused by chemical changes in the composition of sweat.

This is typically followed by a major growth spurt in boys between ages ten and sixteen when their arms, legs, hands, and feet grow faster than the rest of their bodies. Puberty can last anywhere from two to five years, although each child has his or her own unique body composition and chemistry.

Older school-age children are active and extremely energetic with more developed, finer, and larger motor skills. They have a tendency to talk back and be more disobedient and rebellious, which may be their way of imitating older youths or gaining acceptance from their peer group. They need guidance from adults to stay on task

32

and achieve the best results from their efforts. Set limits and let them know what is expected. Give them opportunities to share their thoughts and reactions as they typically view things in the extreme as either black or white.

Proper Education for the Black Child

Black students face a precarious situation as it relates to academic achievement. They perform at comparable levels to their peers in first and second grade, possessing enthusiasm for school and a motivation to learn only to plummet between age eight to thirteen when they recede from the educational process, a phenomenon referred to as the fourth-grade failure syndrome. Education scholar Dr. Jawanza Kunjufu cited the following reasons for the challenges black students (particularly black males) face:

- absence of responsible male role models (a flawed manhood construct, its causal agent)
- the different learning styles of boys and girls
- predominantly female Caucasian teacher population
- inherent bias harbored toward black males
- cultural illiteracy/insensitivity
- disproportionately harsh discipline
- low teacher expectations
- tracking students into special education or remedial instruction despite their capabilities

During preadolescence, children can also be strongly influenced by their peers, sometimes going to great lengths to fit in even if it requires performing poorly. The cumulative effect is further intensified as the socially interactive style of communal and cooperative hands-on learning (preferred by black students) is replaced with a more individualistic, competitive lecture style.

To fill that achievement gap, the Children's Defense Fund (CDF) launched the Freedom Schools Program, which engages servant leader interns and child advocates who prepare program participants to be the next generation to make a difference in themselves and their families as leaders-in-training. Over 150,000 children in K-12 have participated in the CDF Freedom School model with more than seventeen thousand young adults and child allies operating in 182 program sites nationwide. CDF's program roots run deep empowering the young change agents and the communities they serve.

Developmental psychologist Howard Gardner's theory of multiple intelligences differentiates human intelligence as "a biopsychological potential to process information that can be activated in a cultural setting" into eight specific modalities of learning—musical-rhythmic, visual-spatial, verbal-linguistic, logical-mathematical, bodily-kinesthetic, interpersonal-intrapersonal, and existential-moral – an inclusive sensory system that acknowledges and empowers the whole child.

A study that explored teachers' perceptions of intelligence in eleventh-grade black males found that the students were able to perceive their own intelligence in light of Gardner's theory despite the systems in place that undermine black male academic success.[7] Sixty-five years after *Brown v. the Board of Education*, only 69 percent of black students graduate from high school, with the District of Columbia having the highest dropout rate of 94 percent.

> *The drums of Africa still beat in my heart. They will not let me rest while there is a single Negro boy or girl without a chance to prove his/her worth.*

> —Mary McLeod Bethune, educator,
> presidential adviser, civil and women's rights leader

---

[7]   Patrick Anthony Williams, "Exploring Teachers' and Black Male Students' Perceptions of Intelligence" (University of Miami, 2009)

Black girls are being exposed to violence, suspension, expulsion, arrest, hospitalization, and, in the case of ten-year-old Raniya Wright, death under the watchful eyes of teachers and school administrators who prioritize discipline over safety and educational attainment. The very attributes associated with a leader are often deemed inappropriate and punishable if possessed by a black girl. By utilizing punitive, racially based, zero-tolerance policies, these teachers are implicit in the pushouts of black girls whom they've been tasked to educate. Their plight is an untold story. Despite being excluded from existing analysis and research literature related to the school-to-prison pipeline, there is an emerging effort to alleviate the "knowledge desert that exists around the lives and experiences of black girls (and women)." "Black Girls Matter: Pushed Out, Overpoliced and Underprotected," a study published in 2015, examines the various ways girls of color "are channeled into pathways that lead to underachievement and criminalization."

Black girls who are suspended are at disproportionally high risk of being held back, dropping out of school and coming in contact with the juvenile justice system, resulting in severe and long-term consequences that typically lead to a life of disruption and derailment caused by low-wage jobs, unemployment, and living in poverty.

Girlhood Interrupted: The Erasure of Black Girls' Childhood argues that many educators believe black girls are more insubordinate and aggressive and merit less nurturing, protection, support, and compassion reinforced by the theory of adultification, which is a form of dehumanization, robbing them of what makes childhood unique from other developmental life spans.[8]

Citing the work of Subini Annamma, author of *The Pedagogy of Pathologization: Dis/abled Girls of Color in the School-prison Nexus,* the report highlights how black girls as young as five years

---

[8]   Rebecca Epstein, Jamilia J. Blake, and Thalia Gonzalez, *Girlhood Interrupted: The Erasure of Black Girls' Childhood*, Center on Poverty and Inequality (Georgetown Law School, 2017)

old are disciplined for subjective reasons such as exhibiting defiance, noncompliance, or committing minor infractions like dress-code violations or cell phone usage. How justice is experienced and what it should be must be viewed through the eyes of those living the journey.

In the landmark work, *The Pedagogy of the Oppressed*, published nearly fifty years ago, Paulo Freire challenges curricular and pedagogical biases that reinforce systems of domination such as racism and sexism that push children of color into pipelines of violence and incarceration. Freire proposes instead a pedagogy that treats the learner as a cocreator of knowledge whereby education serves as a practice of freedom and a pathway to opportunity and liberation. Freire developed the social concept of *critical consciousness* defining it as "one's ability to transform perceptions and understandings of social and political contradictions in an effort to 'intervene in reality in order to change it.'"

Virtually all states in the nation have adopted restorative justice in some form as a tangible remedy in reducing racial disparities in disciplining. Fania E. Davis—attorney, scholar, and longtime restorative justice practitioner—continues to lead the charge. Davis is the author of *The Little Book of Race and Restorative Justice*, which examines the intersectionality of race and the US criminal justice system and how restorative justice can be the antidote to the centuries-long cycle of prejudice and trauma.

Restorative justice utilizes a culture of connectivity that repairs the harm caused by criminal behavior using equitable and cooperative processes that focus on mediation, agreement, and restitution rather than punishment. All willing stakeholders are offered a seat at the table. The use of restorative justice protocol shifts the focus of discipline from punishment to learning and from the individual to the community. Students learn how to talk (not fight) through their differences by sharing the motivation behind what occurred, which helps both parties better understand the perspective of the other. When a commitment to do better is added, preexisting roadblocks are eliminated.

Capitalizing on the I

G. Stanley Hall asserts that "adolescence is inherently a turbulent time of storm and stress, upheaval and social disorder" that most young people go through before hunkering down in early adulthood and establishing a more stable equilibrium.

The three stages associated with adolescence are early adolescence (age ten to fourteen), middle adolescence (age fifteen to seventeen), and late adolescence (age eighteen to twenty-one).

According to Erik Erikson, the basic conflicts adolescents must face center on developing a strong sense of self and forging an identity that transcends changes in their roles and experiences. Like human pendulums, adolescents swing between extremes—one minute wanting to be surrounded by friends, the next insisting on being alone. The depression and altered mood states that are prevalent during this life span can be worsened by extreme sensitivity, self-criticism or censorship, and seeing the hidden threats that lurk just below the surface.

The propensity to sniff out the inconsistencies and incongruent behaviors of those around them is the adolescents' way of shattering the fixed beliefs of childhood and capitalizing on emergent identity, which defines how they view themselves within diverse contextual experiences.

The craving for novel and intense sensory sensations is particularly heightened during adolescence when monotony, boredom, and routine are deemed intolerable. Adolescents are also acutely susceptible to the influences of media with contemporary social scientists attributing violence, substance abuse, and ethnic/gender stereotypes to music, television, computer/video games, and social media.

The adolescent brain continually changes or rewires itself in response to daily experiences, an adaptation that continues well into the midtwenties. The data associated with screen time—the amount of time spent interacting with TVs, computers, smartphones, digital pads, and video games—and its effect on young minds are still preliminary as scientists attempt to learn whether it causes measurable differences in brain structure and function.

As a precautionary measure, limit your child's access to technology to no more than one to two hours per day. Determine what programming they should consume while at home. Consider deactivating your child's Facebook account as it is "designed to foster addiction, exploiting a vulnerability in human psychology via a social validation content loop," according to Sean Parker, a former Facebook executive.

Criminal behavior peaks at age twelve to fourteen with a distinction between limited, non-preexistent criminal behavior, which has no substantive risk (and can later manifest in productive outcomes that support peer relationships, academic achievement, and school completion) and lifelong criminality (the cumulative effect of poverty, the failure to dispense proper education, accelerated dropout rates) and other nonproductive outcomes that can place adolescents at risk well into adulthood.

The predisposition for violence and other behavioral pathology is racially biased profiling aimed at black girls and boys many of whom already face the trauma and stress meted out daily in America's urban school and on her mean streets. However, none of these scenarios represent the real stories of children fighting to build better futures for themselves and those who help them overcome the challenges they face.

To avoid falling victim to the Cradle to Prison Pipeline, a term coined by attorney and CDF founder, Marian Wright Edelman, parents must take immediate action to ensure their children are aware of this country's racial history and the immorality of ethnic and economic subjugation. This plunge into *darkness* will eventually give way to the *light* of a newly inspired creative, philosophical, and spiritual outlook.

Read and be obsessed with books. Our children need to know where we came from and that we can always find strength, power, and a sense of identity in our culture and shared history. When the cultural and spiritual heritage of our people is fully integrated into our everyday life, we will recover our God-given power and inner divine.

Initiate caring conversations and don't shy away from tackling hot-button topics. *Listen* and *silently* comprise the same letters of the alphabet. Monitor and, if necessary, intervene in any activities and behavior that may place your child in harm's way. There's a purpose in this process. Making this heart-to-heart connection fulfills their need to be authentically seen and heard. Parent-child communication is a key to mutually beneficial well-being.

Encourage their participation in prosocial, culturally relevant activities with teachers and mentors they respect. Young people need someone they can look up to who admires and looks up to them in return.

When they feel stressed or are in a negative headspace, encourage them to *stop* and take slow, deep breaths. To deconstruct the stress, gain composure and assume a calm and meditative stance, encourage them to identify the location of the stress within their body and utilize breathing techniques to balance the stress levels. Flowing with breath and releasing with breath allow for the exhalation of whatever is weighing them down.

Learning effective ways to deal with interpersonal conflict whether with friends, family, or in a confrontation with an authority figure will empower them to accomplish goals, strengthen relationships, and make the passage from childhood to adulthood whole and spiritually, mentally, and physically intact.

The key is to avoid adopting the negative stereotypes associated with this "problematic" life span and, instead, viewing adolescence as a critical transitional period from girl to woman and . . .

. . . Boy to Man

The soul that is within me no man can degrade.

—Frederick Douglass,
culture-bearer, abolitionist, and public intellectual

Frederick Douglass's fearless sense of self, coupled with his incessant commitment to stand in his truth is the embodiment of adolescent attainment. At the age of twelve, a furious fire rose up in him, a blazing obsession that could not be extinguished. His childhood held emancipatory potential, which could not be contained, confounded, comprehended, or coerced. He was tethered—heart and mind— by an absolute and inalienable quest, his "soul aroused to eternal wakefulness." To teach an enslaved man, woman, or child to read was considered an unpardonable offense punishable by fine and imprisonment. But no one would deny Frederick Douglass the right to eat the "valuable bread of knowledge." Come hell or high water, he would stand on the living word of faith and soar in the spirit of hope.

He concocted an ingenious scheme to enlist the help of young Caucasians he met and befriended on the streets of Baltimore. Like them, he was but a boy, and all boys must be bound to someone. "We are linked and interlinked with each other," he once stated.[9]

In exchange for morsels of bread, they taught him and, by their actions, ensured that no one would ever again deny him "the right of learning to read the name of God who made him." Douglass would minister to those young boys on the matter of slavery querying, "Have not I as good a right to be free as you?" And those heartfelt

---

[9]   Frederick Douglass, *Narrative of the Life of Frederick Douglass, An American Slave,* Boston, published at the Anti-Slavery Office, No. 25 Cornhill, 1845

words would tremble within them, and with compassion, they would "console him with the hope that something would occur by which he might be free."

Thus his identity as a masterful orator and fierce emancipationist had been sowed, rooted, and was now bearing good fruit. The virtue associated with this period of adolescence is *fidelity*.

The Columbian Orator, a book on the useful art of eloquence published in 1817, included within its pages a dialogue between a master and slave that would inform Douglass's treatise, giving "tongue to interesting thoughts of his own soul."

This enduring allegiance to his personhood would be revived at age sixteen when Douglass confronted his brutal oppressor/master eye-to-eye, fist-to-fist, and toe-to-toe, beating him within an inch of his life. A developmental process of self-realization that would repeat itself when Douglass escaped to freedom on September 3, 1838, at the age of twenty.

At times it was touch and go. But you made it through. Admit it, you always knew you would. Now it's on to the next quarter—with life's perfect imperfections calling your name. Be assured you have everything within you to effectively answer the call. But first things first . . .

INTRODUCTION TO THE
SECOND QUARTER

Unpack Your Gifts

A man's gift maketh room for him, and
bringeth him before great men.

—Proverbs 18:16 King James Bible

Inhale, exhale, and give thanks for the gift of breath, the cosmic mist of life. Go within, access the gift of belief. Be who you are, achieve what you are capable of, live in your worthiness. Immerse yourself in the gift of culture. Its rich and ancient consciousness is the drumbeat of life. Envision your melanin as a sacred anointing, a gift baptized in the river of the third eye. Now awaken. Tap into your deeper intuition. It is in this moment that all of eternity is contained.

When you unpack your gifts, hold them in the light of day. Sense the deeper presence of the divine burning bright from ember to flame. Imagine the realized potential that is threaded throughout. You are a vessel, a garment, a soulful and sentient song with an ineffable kaleidoscope of colors rhythmically radiating from your chakras, root to crown.

You are an exquisite work of art encrusted with jewels, emeralds, and crystals that reverberate with remembrance, revelation, and reverie. You are an expression of God's one love and one heart, 7.7 billion strong.[10] A diversity of wonders, all that is good, all that is great, and all that is . . . awaits your fervent recognition.

---

[10]   As of August *2019*, the global population is 7.7 billion, according to the most recent United Nations estimates

The talents of an artist, small or great, are God-given . . . Having been given, I must give.

—Paul Robeson, considered one
of the greatest Americans in the twentieth century

Unpacking is the process of opening, unfolding, stretching out, and lifting up layer upon layer of consciousness and before-time prophecies. Your task is to unwrap the boxes within boxes that contain the goodness and godliness that has yet to be revealed. Before you undertake this, listen to the sound of the genuine within you. For to trust and know thyself is to trust and know God.

You were never meant to carry baggage from the past, compartmentalizing segments of your life tucked away in zippered pockets that hold the seconds and moments that create *now*, the only present you can give again and again.

Once upon a time, you knew that love, laughter, and happily ever after would offer what was needed to mine the depths of your inner landscape, excavate, and gather the buried treasure within you that is the individuated version of the Divine. You need not fold yourself to fit into small spaces; you are monumental, a mosaic adornment of the Master.

Share your gifts while you are discovering them. Wrap them with all the passion, purpose, magic, and miracles they hold. Then your gifts will be ready and waiting to present to the world.

Remember, treat every second of your existence as if it were an assignment from God. Everything you do is equally important in his eyes.

THE SECOND QUARTER

Late Adolescence to Early Adulthood (Age 18–35)

Millennials are America's second largest generation with an estimated population of 71 million.

Congratulations, you've gained access to yet another life span. The desire for normalcy is palpable. However, there's no instruction book in sight; you're scripting this narrative intuitively, guiding your vessel in the direction it was preordained to go. Glimpses of a new normal—in the guise of early adulthood—invoke intense feelings of confusion and isolation, but you know you're never alone.

God is in the midst, having bestowed you with a storehouse of gifts—wisdom, understanding, fortitude, knowledge, reverence, a joyful awareness of his grandeur, and the guidance of the Holy Spirit to illuminate his will—and an arsenal of latent artifacts that are being accrued in preparation for this time of reactive response, creativity, and influence.

Teetering between two worlds, you will find balance as you become the temple of your own familiar. The myriad of approaches and responses to this life span are only surpassed by the diversity of roles you can (and will) assume; the combinations are endless.

Your initial unpacking is now complete. The talents you've accumulated thus far have been appraised. You've done the heavy lifting, taking responsibility for who you've discovered yourself to be, evaluating the actions taken and the consequences endured. The questions "Who am I?" and "Where am I going?" still linger. The tender words of Joshua Mack are a prophetic reminder.

It seems like it's a struggle to accept that we are of one original substance. It's not preached and spoken of in the black community as much as faith, hope, and those other inspiring things. We have to get to that place that Wallace B. Wattles spoke of in *The Science of Success: The Secret of Getting What You Want* where he reflects on how we come out of that God substance, that everything is perfect in its own kind. How we address things and how it is reflected back on us is impacted by the media and other sources.

How do we start to build those centers where we help in the evolution of the process and its fulfillment? I think we were placed here to help advance the understanding that everything is as it should be.

The practical aspects of your emerging life require that judgment be reserved. In the interim, be disciplined and discerning. Take your basic instincts and run with them for you have been crowned master of your own cocreation. Calculating the sum total of the unique equation that is you, who's still a work in progress and, as such, is an undertaking to be continuously revisited. Now you must own the better self you aspire to be.

The virtue associated with this life span is *love*; the question to be affirmed is "Am I wanted?" Translate the answer to that inquiry in whatever love language you know best. Whether it entails words of affirmation, acts of service, receiving gifts, quality time, or physical touch, only you can claim who you truly are. Ready yourself. *Now* is the time.

Conscious Adolescence—an Inward Journey

*Don't let anyone look down on you because you are
young, but set an example for the believers in speech,
in conduct, in love, in faith and in purity.*

—1 Timothy 4:12 New International Version

The idealism of late adolescence and its transcendent function have motivated young people across the ages to *fight the power* in pursuit of liberty, justice, and freedom, prompting an acute understanding of not merely what is but the power and pure potentiality that can be tapped into from within.

*All my words that I shall speak unto thee receive
in thine heart, and hear with thine ears.*

—Ezekiel 3:10 King James Bible

In the prime of her youth, Ida B. Wells was called by the Holy Spirit to put pen to paper using words both caustic and corrective to stand up against the lynching and mutilation of men, women, and children, an abomination that prevails even to this day.

Early on, her lord and savior Jesus Christ revealed he had given her the gift of speech and writing to use as a weapon to wage war against those who would perpetuate injustices against African Americans. She adhered to 1 Timothy 4:14 (King James Bible) which states, "Neglect not the gift that is in thee," confident that her gifts might very well set her people free.

Wells aroused the conscience of the masses, demanding that justice would be done though the heavens might fall. Her recorded prayers and conversations with God capture her unceasing faith and deep and abiding love.

"If it were possible, I would gather my race in my arms and fly away. "Oh, God," Wells lamented, "is there no redress, no peace, no justice for us? Show us the way even as thou led the children out of bondage into the Promised Land."

Wells spoke raw, unadulterated truth, unafraid of violent retaliation, relentless in her insistence that there be punishment by law for the lawless even if they characterized themselves as "white."[11]

Like the challenges that Ida B. Wells valiantly faced, late adolescence can present a multitude of quandaries, although a sense of righteousness to "do the right thing" typically prevails due in part to the maturation of higher brain function. In this life span, being kind even in a cruel world takes on added importance. Passion and a deep inner zeal for life represent a significant touchstone in late adolescence. Metathinking that helps modulate the emotions stimulating the ability to work things out in the head *and* in the heart is a metaphoric compass young adults can refer to as they navigate this phase of their life journey.

Conflicts in the transition to adulthood can make passage through the "betwixt and between" difficult, precipitating major life crisis that can manifest in feelings of invisibility (a perpetual "state" of nothingness). A shift from *carefree, self-centeredness* to *responsibility and self-development* must occur as it reinforces social expectations that are internalized, informing the youth's own sense of morality and defining what constitutes honor, fortitude, and good character. A self-realized process that is critical particularly for African American youth as they embark on this extended search for self.

---

[11] Hilda Booker Williams, "Ida B. Wells-Barnett: A Black Feminist Called by God to Influence Social Transformation" (a paper presented at the National Association of African American Studies, February 1999).

What you help a child to love can be more
important than what you help him to learn.

—African proverb

Late adolescence is an ideal time to close ranks and create an atmosphere of honesty, mutual trust, and respect that strengthens the cultural and spiritual connection between your sons and daughters and the village of parents, teachers, elders, and other strong black role models who mirror the knowledge and attributes they will soon acquire (and later master). This is the tribe that has invested in your children. These branches on the family tree have already matured, springing forth unique understandings of the renewal, endurance, expression, passion, imagination, intuition, and transmutation that this coming-of-age journey requires to ensure steady and sustained growth. They are living reminders that family ties once made may bend but cannot break—their roots run deep.

When there are caring and compassionate adults fully engaged in their lives, those in late adolescence can have their spiritual, emotional, physical, and educational needs met and avoid roadblocks that may hinder their climb up the ladder of opportunity. Having the loving presence of others is essential; it guarantees that a strong foundation is built and added onto from one life stage to the next. Yoking them in a meaningful and deeply transformative way to what God has ordained for their life and those of their future sons and daughters.

Here I stand before the threshold to adulthood ready to sever
the ties of my youth, and begin new growth on the dead tree that
represents childhood. The tree of youth that once stood tall with
all its quirky branches and knots, now lays horizontal, ready to
give my new growth all the water and nutrients it needs to grow.

—Eli Keltz, former participant,
Rites of Passage Journeys

Traditional societies throughout Africa mark the adolescent entry into early adulthood with a rites of passage (ROP) composed of complex systems, structures, rituals, and ceremonies by which age-class members (ranging from twelve to nineteen years old) come to know who they are, their relationship to and role in the community, and their link to the broader and more potent spiritual world. In the process, initiates gain a deeper comprehension of their existence from one sphere of reasoning and responsibility to the next. These intentionally ritualized ceremonies, conducted with blessings from respected community elders, play a central role in socialization and are critical in nation building and identity formation.

The initiation process "prepares males for their responsibilities in the community as men and females for their responsibilities in the nation as women."[12] Adulthood rites are only one set within a larger system of rites that also include birth, marriage, eldership, and ancestorship.

For Africans in the US, rites of passage can systematically guide and direct youth in our ancient ways serving as a valuable (and essential) body of knowledge and understanding of the manner in which we can tap into our motherland's origins to train our people up while preserving the community as a symbol of collective permanence. Parents, mentors, and elders "who participate in rites of passage must themselves have been initiated as one cannot teach what one has never been taught."[13]

The rituals and ceremonies of the Ibo of Nigeria mark the phases of life on earth, while the Akan of Ghana conduct rites associated with life crisis. The Senufo of the Ivory Coast initiate girls into the secret women's society of Poro through a process that lasts for a period of seven or eight years. Their initiation rites prominently feature ritual songs, masks, tests/ordeals, tattooing, and a ceremonial dance called

---

[12]   Annika S. Hipple, "Coming of Age Rituals in Africa: Tradition and Change," *Prudence International Magazine*, Fall 2008.

[13]   Manu Ampim, "The Five African Initiation Rites," September 2003. http://www.manuampim.com/AfricanInitiationRites.htm

the Ngoron, the steps of which can take up to six months to master, marking the culmination of the girls' ritual training. These ordeals reflect the belief that pain is an integral part of becoming an adult. Therefore, the youngsters who undergo the agony of such ordeals with courage will be empowered to endure the challenges of life and advance the pride of their people.

Some form of rites of passage accompanies every phase of the human development life span and is indicative of a process, a becoming, and a transformation. These rites serve as an educational cognition marked by three phases: (1) separation (preliminary) symbolic behavior signifying a detachment of the individual or group from a previously held social structure or set of cultural conditions; (2) margin (liminal) a state of ambiguity or disorientation that occurs in the middle stage of rites, when initiates pass through a realm devoid of the attributes associated with their past or forth coming status; and (3) aggregation (postliminal) indicating that the passage is consummated.[14] Now they possess the spiritual, moral, cultural, and societal values required to emerge into adulthood.

Whether informal or formal, rites of passage impart sustainable knowledge imbued with the soul and spirit of a people. When systematically applied, this set of customs, practices, and rituals can speak to and satisfy the yearnings of the initiates' hearts as they live out their destiny as individuals and respected members of the nation.

Cultural Consciousness

Through cultural consciousness, one gains cognizance of the culture's values and traditions whereby an intrinsic awareness within the self is developed, resulting in an expanded understanding of the society in all its contexts. Culture imbues life's practical struggles with a sacred sense of wonder that can intuit the mysteries of life.

---

[14]   Lance Williams, PhD, "The Rites of Passage as a Cultural Retooling Process for Black Youth in their Adolescent-to-Adulthood Transition" in *Black Child Journal.*

For African American youths, cultural pride and positive racial identity translate into adaptive coping mechanisms that heighten self-esteem and increase academic success, which can serve as a protective social function affecting emotional intelligence as well as overall health and well-being.

> *The progress of the world will call for the*
> *best that all of us have to give.*

—Mary McLeod Bethune

The African legacy of paying it forward extends back to antiquity. As witnessed in the works of the "luminous one" Fatima al-Fihri (Fatima bint Muhammad al-Fihriya al-Qurashiya) who, in AD 859, founded the oldest continuously operating, first degree-awarding university on earth, University of al-Qarawīyyīn located in Fès, Morroco, once a leading spiritual and educational center of the Muslim world.

Al-Fihri distinguished herself later in life dedicating her entire inheritance in benevolence to her community. She founded al-Qarawīyyīn Mosque after observing that the local mosques could not accommodate the growing population of worshippers. Extremely devout, al-Fihri fulfilled a religious vow she took to fast daily from the first day of construction to the project's completion two years later, offering prayers of gratitude in the very mosque she had worked to build.

This esteemed institution had eight thousand students by the fourteenth century and even to this day maintains a rigorous selection process requiring every student who applies to have memorized the entire Koran. The university's library, built in AD 1359, is recognized as the oldest in the world housing over four thousand manuscripts, many of which date back to the ninth century.[15]

---

[15] Taylor, Mildred Europa, "The Oldest University Is in Africa and It Was Founded by a Woman," Face2Face Africa, May 22, 2018

Our penchant for gifting is intricately linked to the cultural precept of collective work and responsibility "to build and maintain our community together and to make our brother's and sister's problems our problems and to solve them together" the third principle—Ujima—of Kwanzaa's Nguzo Saba. Research confirms that African Americans typically view their gift of time and money as their responsibility to one another, not monetary donations given to strangers in support of a good cause.

Oseola McCarty exemplifies homegrown giving and its ability to affect change. Conceived when her mother, Lucy, was raped, Ms. McCarty (known as Ms. Ola) was raised by her grandmother and aunt, whom she cared for after dropping out of school in sixth grade. To say she lived a hardscrabble life is a monumental understatement.

She found pride in the provisions God afforded in her work as a laundress stashing the money earned from ironing first in her doll buggy and later in a savings account. At the age of eighty-seven, Ms. Ola donated $150,000 (of her $280,000 life savings) to the University of Southern Mississippi to establish a scholarship fund for worthy but needy students seeking the education she never was afforded. When others learned of this lifelong Mississippians' selfless act, over six hundred men and women made donations that more than tripled her original endowment.

The act of giving is the bedrock of the black church, which is tasked to meet the spiritual, psychological, financial, educational, and humanitarian needs of its members. It's a core institution where benefactors like Ms. Ola give as a form of worship to God.

"I start each day on my knees, saying the Lord's Prayer. Then I get busy about my work," she told one interviewer. "You have to accept God the best way you know how, and then he'll show himself to you. And the more you serve him, the more *able* you are to serve him." This is a moral and ethical compass that guided Oseola McCarty's unique journey of generosity.

Billionaire investor and philanthropist Robert F. Smith's pledge to eliminate student loan debt for the 396 graduating seniors of Morehouse College (class of 2019) was a powerful reminder that we are enough for our community. The gift totaling an estimated $40 million was made on behalf of eight generations of the Smith family and acknowledges the legacy of sharing and caring employed by our foreparents, which has served as our upkeep. "Their struggles, their courage, and their progress allowed me to strive and achieve," Smith wrote in his commencement speech. "It is incumbent on all of us to pay this inheritance forward."

Higher Learning

College, like other institutions of higher learning, is synonymous with and germane to the fulfillment of the developmental factors associated with late adolescence and early adulthood. The focus on independent inquiry and the acquisition, mastery, and application of knowledge creates a synergistic space to freely and fully explore the ever-evolving definitions of *self* that ultimately coalesce into identity.

From a young age, Paul Robeson exemplified the inherent genius of black youth and the hard-earned determination required of those who seek advancement and the God-given right to hold their destiny in their own hands. Born in 1898 to a father who was a runaway slave and later a college graduate and a mother who was raised in an abolitionist Quaker family, at his core, Robeson was his brothers' and sisters' keeper.

A scholar, attorney, actor, singer, and human rights activist, he saw strength, intelligence, and the will to be self-authored articulated in his family, psychological building blocks he used to create a legacy he would never betray.

Robeson was self-actualized, embodying a sense of worthiness and vigilance that widened his sphere of influence and his ability to profoundly impact the world. At every juncture, he achieved what had been deemed unachievable for a young black American man— winning a four-year academic scholarship to Rutgers University and fifteen varsity letters in baseball, basketball, track, and football, serving as valedictorian, graduating from Columbia Law School, and passing the bar—before shifting gears and honing a prolific career in music, theater, and film that would earn him international acclaim. Fighting fascism abroad and racism at home, Robeson vowed to use his global platform to promote the history and culture of Africa and her enslaved descendants.

"The artist must decide where he stands. He must elect to fight for freedom or for slavery. I have made my choice. I had no alternative."

Robeson sang in his deep baritone performing in twenty-five languages "feeding the people with his song" in crowds that numbered thirty thousand to forty thousand. He saw "in peace our most sacred responsibility."

Robeson never wavered, always defining and seeing manifested another identity and reality for black people. Throughout his life, "I must keep fightin' until I'm dying" remained his declaration of resistance.

There would be no lynching if it did not first start in the classroom.

—Carter Godwin Woodson, PhD, historian, educator,
and father of Black History Month

Throughout history, miseducation has profoundly affected the academic advancement and success available to those of African descent whose access to proper elementary education and higher learning has been systematically thwarted.

Carter G. Woodson explored this dynamic in his seminal work *The Mis-Education of the Negro* published in 1933 stating, "Negroes are educated in a system that dismisses them as non-entities and emphasizes their inferiority, a taught bias which when believed hinders their ability to be of service to their people." This evocative work was conceived in the mind of a scholar who toiled in the coal mines of West Virginia before enrolling in high school at the age of twenty, becoming the first and only African American born to slaves to earn a doctorate in history.

Woodson stated that "the function of so-called modern education is to conform to the needs of those

who have enslaved and oppressed weaker peoples based on a philosophy and ethics that reinforce the justification of slavery, segregation, and lynching," a system that induces the oppressor's self-predicated exalted state.

"Therefore, race prejudice is merely the logical result of that tradition, the inevitable outcome of thorough instruction to the effect that the Negro has never contributed anything to the progress of mankind," a flawed construct that Woodson's research and scholarship refutes as does the work of his cohorts Oliver Jones, George Washington Williams, J. T. Wilson, and W. J. Simmons.

Despite our best efforts, racialized rhetoric, language, and pedagogies continue to marginalize, oppress, and silence. Ultimately, we must either choose to live and make peace with an unjust world or come to terms with death and discover what life should truly be. The struggle may continue, but our victory is certain.

Woodson constructed a corrective and restorative narrative that was liberatory as did Paul Robeson through his international activism. Both of whom inculcated in the minds of the black masses, members of the working class, and youths the belief that our psychological and cultural liberation remains intrinsically tied to knowledge of our glorious past.

Carter G. Woodson saw the blessing in our blackness, dedicating his life to the cause ensuring that our accomplishments would stand like twin pillars, monuments that acknowledge our racial heritage and legacy of achievement, divinely appointed gifts that more than justify, assuming our rightful place as the first children of the Most High God.

> *Civilization is in a race between education and catastrophe. Let us learn the truth and spread it as far and wide as our circumstances allow. For the truth is the greatest weapon we have.*
>
> —H. G. Wells, author

Huey P. Newton, cofounder with Bobby Seale of the Black Panther Party for Self-Defense, alluded to the miseducation of black youth in his autobiography, *Revolutionary Suicide*. A staunch advocate of lifelong learning, Newton rose from a high school graduate unable to read going on to earn a doctorate in social philosophy using his philosophical inclinations to unite the academy with the street.

> During those long years in Oakland public schools, I did not have one teacher who taught me anything relevant to my own life or experience. Not one instructor ever awoke in me a desire to learn more or to question or to explore the worlds of literature, science, and history. All they did was try to rob me of the sense of my own uniqueness and worth and, in the process, nearly killed my urge to inquire.

One of the most degrading things you can subject someone to is not caring about their mind.[16] Teacher and educational activist Marva Collins disproved the notion that black children possess a natural capacity to fail, stating instead that it is the teachers, the school systems in which they work, and those who teach the children they are failures that pose the most critical problem.

---

[16]   Sofia Lundberg, *The Red Address Book* (New York: Houghton Mifflin Harcourt, 2017)

When black students (particularly males) enter college, their sense of pride and self-esteem can easily shift focus from academic engagement and achievement to peer popularity and athletics, lessening the importance of academic identity versus overall self-definition, what social psychologist Claude Steele refers to as academic dis-identification.[17]

When they perceive they're being viewed through the lens of a negative stereotype, a fear of doing something that inadvertently confirms that stereotype occurs. For African American students, this stereotype threat can impact all academic arenas affecting test scores, college grades, graduation rates, and academic identity as a whole and can easily invoke covert intimidation to their psyche a constant reminder that they are always walking on thin ice and are subject to fundamental disadvantages attributable to racial/ethnic bias.

Despite the fact that black student graduates tend to do just as well in professional attainment as their collegiate peers, they still need to be proactive, consciously casting aside all insecurities that compromise their understanding of the historical power, traditions, and doctrines that have sustained our people across generations and geography.

We come from a culture of achievement where young, gifted, and black students' inherent brilliance empowers them to surpass, equal, and excel. In the words of Marva Collins, "I will is more important than IQ." Educators must do their part by creating a culture of excellence where learning takes precedence and academic accomplishment is the norm.

---

[17]   Karen Powell Sears, "Extending Disidentification Theory: The Effects of Stereotype Threat on the Self-Concept, Academic Engagement, and School Performances of African American and Latino High School Students," 2005.

A Mind Is a Terrible Thing to Waste

Between doubt and your destiny is action. Between our community and the American dream is your leadership. You . . . are bound only by the limits of your conviction and creativity.

—Robert F. Smith, entrepreneur, technology investor, and philanthropist

Alexander Lucius Twilight was the first African American to graduate from a college in the US, earning his bachelor's degree from Middlebury College in 1823 going on to become a minister, educator, and the first black elected to public office in 1836 affirming the "ability of the common person to rise to an exalted state through hard work and talents." The nation's first black public high school, Paul Laurence Dunbar High, named after the Harlem Renaissance poet laureate, opened its doors in Washington, DC, in 1870.

Historically black colleges and universities (HBCUs) have played an integral role in the education, self-realization, and generational success of African American students over its long and illustrious history. These institutions of academic excellence were first established in the south as a result of the second Morrill Land-Grant Act of 1890 that "donated public lands to states and territories which provided colleges for the benefit of agricultural and mechanical arts." Sixteen exclusively black colleges and universities were awarded 1,890 land-grant funds.

Several of those institutions had already been established by that point with the oldest being Cheyney University of Pennsylvania (1837), University of District of Columbia (1851), Lincoln University (1854), Wilberforce University (1856), Harris-Stowe University (1857), Shaw University (1865), and Tuskegee University (1881), which opened the way for more HBCUs to be established.

In title III of the Higher Education Act of 1965, Congress coined the term *HBCU* defining it as "a school of higher learning that was accredited and established before 1964, and whose principal mission was the education of African Americans." As of 2015, nearly three hundred thousand students have attended HBCUs.[18]

Currently, there are 101 HBCUs in the US, including public and private institutions. Howard University, Hampton University, Spelman College, Fisk University, Morehouse College, Tuskegee University, and Dillard University are considered the academic crème de la crème of the black Ivy League.

HBCUs graduate the who's who of black innovators and influencers—such as Dr. Martin Luther King Jr., Marian Wright Edelman, Langston Hughes, Alice Walker, Toni Morrison—and millennial innovators, disruptors, influential startup execs, and politicians, such as Diishan Imira, Rosalind G. Brewer, Jamarlin Martin, Janice Bryant Howroyd, Katrina Turnbow, Marilyn Mosby, and Arlan Hamilton, founder and managing partner of Backstage Capital just to name a few.

HBCUs are now experiencing a resurgence, a black renaissance, as students seek safe havens, where in the midst of self-discovery, they can also be academically challenged yet still inspired to grow.

Research from the Gallup organization shows that graduates of HBCUs report better college experiences than African American students who attend white academic institutions and are twice as likely to agree that their university prepared them well for life outside academia with everything designed to contribute to their long-term success.

In their quest to prosper the world to its fuller expression, first-year black college students are seeking admittance into HBCUs in their search for equity and justice for all rather than compliance and submission for the few. HBCUs reflect a world where black lives have always mattered.

---

[18] Pew Research Center analysis of fall enrollment data from the US Department of Education National Center for Education Statistics

Looking for the ideal HBCU has never been easier thanks to tech phenom Jonathan Swindell, a Grambling State University graduate whose brainchild, the HBCU Hub, is a free mobile app that helps high school students navigate through the entire college application process in preparation for gaining acceptance into their dream-come-true HBCU. Through the app, students can find information on scholarships, participate in an online chat community, get tips on writing winning résumés, and acing job interviews. With a commitment to break the cycle of underrepresentation in education, HBCU Hub is motivated by a modest principle: an educated black person *can* take over the world.

Equal access to a college education is the key to success. For African Americans, however, it may be a double-edged sword frayed with economic risks that may threaten long-term financial stability. According to a study titled "Racial Disparities in Student Debt and the Reproduction of the Fragile Black Middle Class," student loan debt is racialized and disproportionately affects black youth, widening the wealth gap between college-going Caucasians and African Americans across the early adult life span. The authors conclude that student debt may be a new mechanism of wealth inequality that creates fragility in the next generation of the black middle class.

While student loan repayment and education debt is a concern for all college student borrowers, African Americans incur the most with 85 percent more debt than Caucasians because of challenging repayment options for students whose families have lower income. The study notes that while black youths have been given more access over the past years, they have made those gains on exploitative terms, described as predatory inclusion.

"The racial wealth gap is both the biggest and has grown the fastest among those with a college education," explains Jason Houle, a coauthor of the study. "We point to student loan debt as potentially one thing that explains why that's happened."

Emerging Adulthood

Financial independence, accepting personal responsibility, and making decisions apart from other influences are no longer the typical markers indicative of impending adulthood. In Westernized cultures, the majority of those aged eighteen to twenty-five undergo what psychologist Jeffrey Jensen Arnett calls emerging adulthood, an ambiguous waiting period marking the shift from adolescence to early adulthood.

Arnett theorizes there are five stages associated with this developmental life span: self-focus, instability, identity exploration, feeling in-between, and a sense of possibilities.

Identity: Lost and Found

One of the main struggles emerging adults face is the lingering sense of lost identity and self-definition caused in part by the "leave it to chance" approach to adulthood development, the primary root of confusion, inner turmoil, and uncertainty that occurs in this life span.

Emerging adults spend more time alone than any population with the exception of the elderly. Although the most technologically connected generation in the history of the world, they are extremely isolated, viewing life through the lens of social media–induced obsessive comparison disorder (the new OCD), a fictitious phenomenon. They are both the master of and a servant to.

The pressure to find the right occupation can be overwhelming as emerging adults find themselves not fitting into the culture and climate of today's work environments. In our highly competitive global world, undergraduate degrees—coupled with exorbitant, financially crippling student debt—only go so far, furthering the need to acquire more schooling and advanced training, thus delaying an already fragile sense of stability. As a result, those in this life span may find themselves "switching jobs nearly every year for a decade."

Even when they are not ascending a crystal stair, the urge (for those in this life span) is to keep climbing and explore all the dead ends, wrong turns, stop signs, and near collisions they've maneuvered through. Many use external success and accolades to define self-worth, a subjective assessment that may lull them into believing they're either measuring up or falling short. On one hand, self-esteem is boosted; on the other hand, validation of the ego is being sought.

Embrace the intensity that marks this search for personal authenticity, awareness, and self-definition. Have the courage to confront any self-doubt and maximize the frequent need for introspection by taking a closer look. Face the crises of the mind and spirit that a college education rarely prepares you for. It's not about how you look, your net worth, who you know, what you do, or ultimately, what you achieve.

The quarter life is about really getting real with yourself, working through the chaos and upheaval and finding a way to feel good about who you are right now, an important process in this emotionally charged life span. In the interim, give yourself permission to confront the principle behind this "failure to launch."

Conscious Early Adulthood

Early adulthood with all its newfangled commitments and residual confusion can stimulate a deep desire to gain awareness (and find solutions) to life's many complexities. Lacking significant signposts that usher in its onset, this life span can galvanize a young person to tap into their innate ability to work out the kinks and conditions of the past in preparation for the future.

On the positive side, this can be a period of great enterprise with new responsibilities to be accomplished—work, social relationships, marriage, and children—with person-building being the most formidable.

Despite boundaries between childhood and adulthood that are often blurred, those in the midst of this life span need only to walk the walk and put their words into action—behavior that Christopher Gardner mirrored as he placed one foot in front of the other, moving into his purpose with unwavering intention. The twenty-seven-year-old struggled with homelessness but was never hopeless raising his toddler son in flophouses and on the streets of San Francisco in pursuit of the "happyness" that comes when your accomplishments reflect your dreams.

Gardner counted the baby steps, looked back, and when he added them up, discovered he had aligned his life with his values, creating a profound sense of contentment and meaning through his work as a businessman, investor, stockbroker, motivational speaker, author, and philanthropist earning him a stunning net worth of over $60 million. His was an epic journey with rewards that far outweighed the challenges faced and overcame.

Toltec tradition advises to always use the power of your words in the direction of truth and love. "Others may question your credentials, your papers, your degrees or look for all kinds of ways to diminish your worth. But never hesitate to claim your dreams. What is inside you no one can take from you or tarnish."

This developmental phase is characterized by peak physical abilities including muscle strength, reaction time, sensory abilities, and cardiac functioning. However, the aging process begins at this time with changes in skin, vision, and reproductive capability. When automatic function is out of alignment with the circadian rhythm, sleep can be disrupted, affecting the formation of melatonin. This

further exacerbates neurological toxins emitted from the cell phones/
technology, which would normally be removed naturally by the body.

Our bodies communicate with us at all times. Listen intuitively and
put what you are being told into practice, so the frequency can shift
and balance can be restored.

Mi Casa En Su Casa

Young adults who leave home and attend college report greater
affection, communication, and satisfaction in their relationships with
their parents, providing an opportunity for transformation even in
their relation with siblings who may experience new responsibilities
and privileges associated with their change in status.

Exiting the home front is an important first step young women tend
to undertake earlier than their male counterparts many of whom
experience "umbilical whiplash," which interrupts the call to
independence. The dreams of women who hold up half of the sky
are often circumvented by the push to marry and start a family rather
than supported as they venture into the world to make their mark.

Approaching this new stage of growth with optimism and intention
will help them muster the courage to declare, "This is my life. It's up
to me to move in the direction that best suits my gifts and capabilities."
Getting serious about the rest of their life may require them to put on
their thinking caps. Advise them to work out a resolution between
their own ideals and those you hold as their parents, and factor in their
unique perception of what the world demands. Lessening the pain
from the parental split may require them to look for other options.
Joining the military or the Peace Corp, becoming a missionary, tutor,
or au pair are worthy short-term vocations that may temporarily fill
the achievement gap.

During early adulthood, the duality of good/bad and right/wrong and all sensibilities of adolescence merge into a "whatever works or whatever's clever" attitude as a new type of pragmatism emerges. Explore and discover ways to assist them in fulfilling their personal dreams. Knowing they are of extraordinary significance can powerfully alter their worldview. Their innate talents can be easily translated into professional opportunities that will inspire a true sense of accomplishment, leading them toward a path to greatness. Encourage them to take full advantage of every opportunity to build on those talents.

Predictable stages of psychological development also occur during adulthood yet another time in which one seeks to engage with one's own consciousness. The mind continues its pursuit of happiness, meaning, and enlightenment as a part of growth and functionality, guiding the individual (if they choose) on a path to serenity and fulfillment.

Advise them to give their best because others will rarely tolerate the leftovers.[19] Everything around them is a product of who they are. In the end, it's all about the business of becoming their authentic selves. The options they choose can set the tone for the life they live now and in the future.

Conscious Abundance

Give generously to them and do so without a grudging heart;
then because of this the LORD your God will bless you in
all your work and in everything you put your hand to.

—Deuteronomy 15:10 New International Version

There are 20.9 million sixteen- to twenty-four-year-olds in the workforce,[20] each actively engaged in key developmental tasks

---

[19] Simon T. Bailey, "Don't Let Your Ladder Be Propped Against the Wrong Wall," by Goalcast, June 18, 2018.

[20] US Bureau of Labor Statistics, July 2018.

(decision-making, building social skills, mastering new levels of responsibility, and acquiring knowledge) that ensure healthy development throughout this life span. Research shows that working during high school lowers dropout rates, improves career prospects, and ensures higher salaries, a sound investment that pays dividends well into the future.

Alongside gratifying relationships, establishing a professional career is one of the foremost requirements for sustaining a fulfilled life. Discernment comes into play as those in this life span discover their true talents and make sense of their desires and who they aspire to be. When they acknowledge who they truly are, what they have to offer, and how that energy should be directed, they can shine their light on the world, and in the process, never have to work a day in their life.

Paving the Road to Economic Freedom

Nineteenth-century black business owners—men and women alike—set the standard for entrepreneurial excellence. For example, titans like Samuel T. Wilcox, who established the first high-quality grocery store that amassed annual sales in the millions; and Stephen Smith, an indentured servant who toiled in lumberyards before buying his freedom for fifty dollars and later going on to establish a lumber and coal business, yielding him a net worth equivalent to $13.5 million; Clara Brown, who established a successful laundry business during the Colorado gold rush, creating a diverse portfolio of real estate investments; and Frederick Patterson, the first African American to manufacture a car—the Patterson-Greenwood—direct competition to the Model T. The Independent Order of St. Luke (IOSL) opened a bank in 1903, which is the longest-operating black-controlled financial institution until its sale in 2011.

Historically, blacks have always put their shoulders to the wheel, and despite American workplace apartheid, they surpassed their Caucasian contemporaries, making a way out of no way.

"For us, by us" could best describe the golden age of black entrepreneurship, which spanned from 1900 to 1930, a stellar time when black business elite catered to black clientele traversing numerous industries including financial services, retail, media, beauty, and entertainment.

Booker T. Washington saw the efficacy in promoting black-owned enterprises, founding the National Negro Business League (NNBL) in 1900. Eventually, Washington opened over six hundred chapters inspiring numerous offshoot associations and corporations. According to the NNBL, the number of black-owned businesses doubled from twenty thousand in 1900 to forty thousand in 1914. The most substantial increase was seen in retail merchants, which nearly tripled from ten thousand to twenty-five thousand.

Thomas Moss, founder of the People's Grocery; Robert Abbott, publisher of *Chicago Defender*; Maggie Smith, founder of St. Luke's Penny's Bank; and John Merrick, founder of North Carolina Mutual Insurance Company represent a sampling of black business nobility who faced down racial hostility, violence, thievery, and economic exclusions only to rise and carry on yet another day.

At the turn of the century, a family of four could survive on an annual salary of $312 (the equivalent of less than $9,000 in 2016), most of which when combined with savings went toward home ownership. An honest depiction of black life at that time juxtaposes the harsh reality of discrimination and poverty with the collective determination of a people for whom prospects went hand-in-hand with progress. Slow and steady always wins the race.

It's not the type of season for backing down/ You have to see your Ancestors in broad daylight.

—Tongo Eisen-Martin, movement worker and poet

Like the black entrepreneurs who were her predecessors, Madam C. J. Walker (Sarah Breedlove) stood on her own ground, and by her own hand "got her start by giving herself a start," thereby establishing a beauty culture that would revolutionize the black hair care and cosmetic industry. Unapologetic, she claimed a divine calling God revealed to her in a dream that propelled her from earning $1.50 a day to millionaire status as one of the twentieth century's most successful, self-made entrepreneurs.

Born on the plantation where her parents had been enslaved, Walker was orphaned at age seven, married at age fourteen, widowed by age twenty, and overcame formidable obstacles that were no match for her tenacity and unceasing belief first in God and then in herself. Walker and the thousands of beauty culturalists she employed embraced a "lift as we climb" philosophy that would fuel her rags-to-riches ascent. "There is no royal flower-strewn path to success. If I have accomplished anything in life, it is because I have been willing to work hard."

Make no mistake about it, black people have always been the boss and consistently pay the cost—with over 2.6 million African American–owned businesses in 2018, most of which are owned by black women ages thirty-five to fifty-four.

An Inside Job

Believing is seeing when it comes to accessing the abundant success awaiting you. Spending quality time zooming in on your assets is a reminder of those things you love about yourself and the new paths God will help you take. Gifting this next level of self-love is the greatest present you can receive, allowing you to make peace with the *now* as you prepare for the satisfaction that comes with achieving the *later*. You are good enough, capable enough, and lovable enough to live your best life now.

Recognize opportunities and take the wins where you can get them. Put the pedal to the metal and invest in your success. Missing the mark isn't a sin; take another shot and hit the bull's eye. Add value and do something a little extra. Consistency always pays off; it leads to bigger and better. Never forfeit your dreams. Ingenuity will take you to high places. "There's no such thing as failure. You either win, or you learn."

Resist any urge to compare yourself to others. Criticism is never a vehicle through which you can journey to self-love. Be meticulous in your self-scrutiny, and don't fall prey to the imposter syndrome. The fear of failure and being "found out" can sabotage your efforts to reach your full potential. You are wonderful, unique, and a human capable of succeeding in any situation you can imagine. If need be, have a come-to-Jesus chat with you inner critic and put all poor-me sensibilities on pause.

Embarking on a job search is a daunting, difficult, stressful, and unavoidable part of transitioning into the real world. Preparing yourself mentally and spiritually for the necessary work ahead is a positive prerequisite. Go, go, go—time is of the essence.

Once you've found a job/opportunity that piques your interest, immediately move into research overdrive. Create a success model that is unconventionally you. Do your homework; show what you know about the company, the people it employs, and how you will be a perfect fit. Bank on yourself, avoid the "better luck next time" pitfalls and show you're ready, willing, and raring to go.

Success has many parents, failure is an orphan.

—Count Caleazzo Ciano, Italian diplomat

Network it up! Don your inner sleuth. Unearth the hidden treasures. Make a list of companies that employ a culture that is personally meaningful to you, one you'd feel honored to contribute to. When culture serves as a company's guiding principles, it's the glue that keeps it and its employees happily bound.

Keep your employment pipeline open. No job is the only job; everyone risks rejection until the right opportunity comes along. Establish a human connection; people who hire people were once sitting right where you are now, a résumé and cover letter away from changing their professional status. Accept, acknowledge, and appreciate where you are. Maintain an attitude of gratitude. You've embarked on the first step knowing your journey will eventually take you a thousand miles from where you now stand.

You know your gifts, having spent your early years fine-tuning them in the presence of your village. Stay inspired and mentally prospered, and be ready to move into the next possibility. Hone your own definition of perfection. Pat yourself on the back for the valiant effort you've made and how far you've come.

If growing your own business aligns with your values, up the ante, be bold, and share your dreams. People will go the distance to help you achieve them. Let them know what they can do, then move out of the way! James 4:2 (King James Version) says, "Yet You have not because you ask not."

Leveling the Playing Field

Antiblack racism needs no life support; it's alive and well, particularly in one crucial life-span area—jobs. Racial bias is hardwired into the hiring process with prejudice negatively affecting those who is deemed a qualified candidate and whose résumé gets tossed. It is a behind-closed-doors predatory practice that is just as strong for businesses that claim to value diversity as those who don't. It is a prevailing method of exclusion that can easily derail careers that would otherwise be on the rise.

"A bias against minorities runs rampant through the résumé screening process at companies throughout the US," according to research by Katherine DeCelles, who further asserts that job applicants who delete references to their race on résumés are twice as likely to get job callbacks, boosting their shot at gainful employment.

Despite achievements in industries from art to war, African Americans are still viewed as not smart enough, not qualified enough, not connected enough, or not good enough—an assessment that's often based on ethnicity. Stephanie Lampkin, a graduate of Stanford and MIT, was all too familiar with the difficulties faced when one doesn't resemble the prototypical applicant. Lampkin is the founder and CEO of Blendoor, a recruiting application that conceals candidates' names and photos as well as information on race, age, gender, or social class to mitigate unconscious bias in hiring. Lampkin's mission is to "challenge the assumption that homogeneous environments are a meritocracy" while demonstrating that investing in diversity yields positive returns across the social, financial, and technological landscape.

While whitening up your résumé may be the new way to get your foot in the door, many are opposed to the bleaching-out trend, choosing to purposely reference culture and ethnicity as an asset rather than a liability. Changing the way companies go about the business of hiring is a slow and grueling process. Lampkin maintains the perspective that the "struggle is far from over. We have a long way to go."

Promoting Healthy Relationships

Research has shown that young African American males attribute four qualities to the development and maintenance of healthy dating relationships: trust, communication, general connection/

compatibility, and respect. [21] Trust was thought to be the most important quality without which there would be no point in dating or establishing a relationship. *Honesty* was defined as "not playing games, being authentic, and willing to tell each other everything."

Communication was the second most important quality whether experienced through technology, cell phones (voice and text), social media, and face-to-face interactions. They believed that the ability to be open, easy, and regular could support a couples' willingness to assist each other with personal issues and serve as an effective tool in resolving conflict. Being able to express what bothers a couple is healthy for the relationship.

In terms of connection and compatibility, the African American males surveyed felt it was important to be with someone who understood them and was willing to be present and who was smart, career-driven, and willing to connect both emotionally and physically. However, they often confused sexual feelings with genuine intimacy.

Querying adolescents, both male and female, on what they should look for in healthy dating relationships open the door to conversations on the qualities needed to develop and sustain wholesome, fulfilling, and everlasting kinships and marriages that can stand the test of time.

The Power of Black Love

> *Love has to be shown by deeds not words.*
>
> —Swahili proverb

---

[21] Donna Howard, Claude John, Brian Gilchrist, Irwin Royster, and Nancy Aiken, "Adolescent African American Males' Characterizations of Healthy Dating Relationship: A Challenge to One-Dimensional Stereotypes," *Journal of Child and Adolescent Behavior* (Department of Behavioral and Community Health, University of Maryland School of Public Health, 2015).

Entering long-term romantic partnerships during early adulthood becomes a crucial undertaking. According to Erik Erikson, selecting a mate is the single most important task of this life span.

Historically, African Americans have been bound together—heart to heart, bone to bone, and soul to soul—willingly creating their own definitions of what constitutes a monogamous spousal relationship, standing their ground and rejecting the conventional matrimonial narrative. These ancestors created unions based on mutual consent, association, and cohabitation that embodied the spirit and meaning they attributed to this fusion of the male and female principle.

They took tremendous pride in their right to lovemaking—a covenant to God, themselves, their families and communities that they would collectively give tongue to marital vows that sanctified their union and spoke a truth that could be translated from generation to generation. African Americans consistently challenged the teleological emphasis on male superiority interspersing it with patterns of matrofocal family organized around the mother. Many choose to reenter slavery to preserve the connection to their beloved who remained in bondage, maintaining the allegiance to community and kinship seen in African societies rather than the narrow Victorian version of family, which destabilized those extended networks. Black adolescents and young adults often lack knowledge and understanding on the positive and empowering perspectives their foreparents historically maintained.

At their best, relationships between black men and women signify strength and commitment to family although pathological stereotypes and their paradoxical nature typically take center stage when such discussions are initiated. Due, in part, to the commodification of the black body reinforced by stereotypical archetypes that depict black females as "sassy, emasculating, and domineering" and black males as "obedient, servile, and lascivious," rhetorical devices that continue to inform African American's social and legal status. Through deeper inquiry, we better understand the dynamics (and impact) of the two-parent, nuclear family as building blocks for the postbellum sharecropper system that guaranteed the labor not only of the black man as head of household but also his wife and children. It is a system that destabilized extended kinship networks with the outmigration of unmarried African American women who had no place to go.

In an effort to establish a vision of family and provide and protect our communities, African Americans have been placed in harm's way. Our love has been maligned, subverted in ways that have ruptured our hearts and severed our belief in one another. Fortunately, positives can always come out of negatives. The diversity in our legacy of love once nourished our minds, bodies, and souls, and with conscious intention, it can do so once again. As we embark on this s/hero's journey, we must acknowledge our capacity to overcome and take the responsibility to reinvent the body, mind, and soul of our love, committing to heal and grow together for "a season, a reason, or a lifetime."

Rite of Marriage

The rite of marriage represents not only the joining of two families but also the comingling of a couple's two missions to ensure their life purposes are fulfilled. The merging of two lives into one is for the purpose of procreating and the perpetuation of life. Of major significance is the coming together of families. The rite of marriage supersedes the notion that falling in love can be the basis of a balanced and sustainable relationship and challenges the relevancy of love at first sight. The emphasis must be placed on the building of families and communities with the focus on the collective as opposed to the individual. In African society, a person must go through rites of passage and will reach adulthood only after they have married and had children.

Healing Together

Let us be aware of our power to create a dream
of heaven where everything is possible.

—Don Miguel Ruiz, author, *The Mastery of Love*

Human beings are hardwired to follow the belief systems held by their families. So much of what is believed (and lived out) in relationships is based on patterns of feelings and behaviors that have been witnessed with our bodies, retaining data received from the sense organs. Episodic, autobiographical information is stored in the right side of the brain and factual information in the left side.

Research has revealed that our earliest relationships, especially those with our mothers, have a large impact not only on how we connect with other adults—be it friends, colleagues, or romantic partners—but plays an integral role in our models of how relationships should work.

A study conducted by Glenn Geher found that human beings are unconsciously drawn toward the familiar and that partners are chosen because they share similar characteristics and adhere to the same internalized scripts as the opposite-sex parent. Invariably, we love in our partner what we (believe we) lack in ourselves. Males unconsciously seek replicas of their mothers, and for females, younger versions of their fathers.

In African culture, the male and female must fulfill three functions for their mate. The man's wife must adhere to the role of mother, sister, lover, and the woman's husband that of a father, brother, and lover. This makes it perfectly acceptable (at least, in African culture) to address their significant others as papa or mama.

When such partnerships occur, the generational cycle of trauma and pain that's embedded on the souls of the descendant can easily be triggered. It is a deep emotional wound that informs the ways in which families live out either heaven or hell right here on earth. The cumulative effects of unconscious pain have the ability to either sever relationships at their root or restore them by a dispensation of trust, honesty, respect, communication, loyalty, happiness, compromise, and safety that will nourish the new growth.

Bell hooks connects black women's difficulties with the "act and art of loving" to their emotional incarceration and the never-ending grief resulting from slavery, a legacy of our stolen personhood. Like the formation of a pearl within an oyster, we have been subjected to intense pressure. As we seek to remove the foreign substance, we often fail to see that the longer that irritant prevails, the larger our greatness (and exquisite beauty) has become.

We must be willing to examine, dissect, and articulate the complexities inherent in our relationships, begin healing our individual and collective trauma, and mentally deconstruct white supremacist ideologies. The retroactivity of those scars sustained as an aftermath of slavery, black codes, Jim Crow, and racial discrimination illicit behaviors that arrest the development and actualization of our divine and higher selves.

All the while, those who characterize themselves as white continue to appropriate (and act out) what they have demonized in passive-aggressive ways that "avow and disavow, attract and repel, and are fixed yet malleable."[22]

An examination of this importance must begin by acknowledging the spiritual, psychological, and physical loss we've suffered and the impact it's had on the manner in which we relate as a people.

Joy DeGruy's theory of post-traumatic slave syndrome (PTSS) delineates the causation of the survival behaviors, mechanisms, and

---

[22]   E. Patrick Johnson, scholar

conditions afflicting African American throughout the US and the diaspora. Maladaptive behaviors resulting from the suffering and traumas inclusive of the periods of capture, transport, enslavement, emancipation leading up to contemporary times.

Her findings represent twelve years of quantitative and qualitative research published in the book *Post Traumatic Slave Syndrome: America's Legacy of Enduring Injury and Healing*. PTSS is an outcome of the multigenerational oppression endured by enslaved Africans and their descendants, resulting from centuries of chattel slavery predicated on the false belief that blacks are inherently or genetically inferior. Thus resulting in MAP:

- **M**—Multigenerational trauma combined with continued oppression;
- **A**—Absence of opportunity to heal or access the benefits available in the society; leading to
- **P**—Post-traumatic slave syndrome

Key patterns of behavior reflective of PTSS include the following:

- Vacant esteem—the insufficient development of primary esteem resulting in feelings of despair, depression, and an overall self-destructive outlook.
- Marked propensity for anger and violence—feelings of suspicion and assigned negativity to the motivations of others accompanied by violence against self, property as well as friends, relatives, or acquaintances.
- Racist socialization and (internalized racism)—learned helplessness, literacy deprivation, distorted self-concept, antipathy or aversion for one's own identified cultural/ethnic group, and the customs, mores, and physical characteristics associated with the group.

Trauma did not end for blacks after slavery. According to DeGruy, "One hundred and eighty years of the middle passage, 246 years of slavery, rape, and abuse; one hundred years of illusionary freedom. black codes, convict leasing, Jim Crow, all codified by our national institutions. Lynching, medical experimentation, redlining, disenfranchisement, grossly unequal treatment in almost every aspect of our society, brutality at the hands of those charged with protecting and serving. Being undesirable strangers in the only land we know. During the three hundred and eighty-five years since the first of our ancestors were brought here against their will, we have barely had time to catch our collective breath." [23] DeGruy further asserts that colorism, black "infighting," materialism, inadequate parenting, jealousy, defeatism, frustration, and rage are the "dysfunctional and negative behaviors" related to transgenerational adaptations associated with past traumas of slavery and ongoing oppression that largely fashions black behavioral and genetic deficiencies."

While the legacy of enslavement may remain etched in the souls of black people, so is the God-frequency and cosmological knowledge of the ancient ones.

Strange Fruit

That the Negro American has survived at all is extraordinary—a lesser people might simply have died out, as indeed others have . . . But it may not be supposed that the Negro American community has not paid a fearful price for the incredible mistreatment to which it has been subjected over the past three centuries.

—Daniel Patrick Moynihan, senator, sociologist, and author, *The Negro Family: The Case for National Action*

---

[23]   Joy DeGruy, *Post Traumatic Slave Syndrome: America's Legacy of Enduring Injury and Healing*, revised ed., (Joy Degruy Publications Inc., September 11, 2017), pp. 107–108.

African Americans born in the 1980s are more likely to experience the loss of a mother in early childhood, a father through their midteens, a sibling in their teens, and a child by age thirty, and are 90 percent more likely to experience four or more deaths by age sixty-five, according to a study by the Population Research Center at the University of Texas at Austin, the first population-based documentation of bereavement experiences for black Americans.

"The potentially substantial damage to surviving family members is a largely overlooked area of racial disadvantage," according to the study's lead author, Debra Umberson, who is also a sociology professor and the center's director.

Deadly diseases like diabetes, asthma, cancer, sarcoidosis, and stroke disproportionately affect African American's pathology and exacerbate their quality of life. The psychopathology of race-based stress is also an antecedent to elevated heart disease. All of which further accelerates the negative physiological and psychological consequences. The end result is an intergenerational cognitive process that over time disrupts the psyche of African American families and communities.

African Americans die at a much higher rate than Caucasians. The evidence of racial disparities in life expectancy and mortality risk in the United States is long-standing and irrefutable, the study states.

"This is a tragedy, one that reverberates throughout these family networks to affect many people in ways that surely take a toll on their lives," Umberson adds. "There should be interventions and strategies that address grief, bereavement, and loss."

Poverty, criminal victimization/mass incarceration, inadequate health care, and the legacy of environmental racism can be directly linked to the system of racism, white supremacy, which adversely impacts those of African descent across the globe.

"We must recognize there are some arbitrary issues that are present in the way we practice medicine and dole out health care," said Clyde W. Yancy, MD, associate dean of clinical affairs and medical director for heart failure/transplantation at the University of Texas Southwestern Medical Center.

For blacks, dying and death is not a phenomenon that solely afflicts the elderly. It's far more complex than the pervasive images seen in the media. The mental, physical, and spiritual toll it takes precipitates a level of loss, abandonment, and grief that is immeasurable. We have been at risk across the life span. Untimely death and dying continues to mark our experience.

Thoughts of the life we should be leading must take center stage in our consciousness. In the words of author Richard Wright, "We must do something to redeem our being alive." Disrupt the status quo. Employ strategic prayer and fasting vigils. Organize a massive (mental) boycott. Demand that the flagrant disregard for our human rights be brought into immediate correction.

The habitual disruption and strain in the formation, duration, and quality of our kinship systems/relationships and mental and physical health must be remedied immediately. The fracture of social connections that are essential to human development and fundamental to human health must undergo reparations. We must be vigilant so that our long-term futures are not further compromised.

We are not our trauma and pain. We embody earthly jewels of knowledge, a treasure trove of talents that illuminate our collective genius. We must return to our right minds and gain back our senses. Ultimately, the darkness cannot comprehend or withstand our light.

The choice is ours alone. Let us access God's inextricable love in all that we endeavor to undertake.

INTRODUCTION TO THE
THIRD QUARTER

Take Turns Taking the Lead

*If you want to go quickly, go alone. If you
want to go far, go together.*

—African proverb

Taking turns (simultaneous sharing) is the first step in creating mutually beneficial interactions. It represents the most basic, back-and-forth rhythm that occurs in everyday exchanges. As you mature, taking turns can become a way of giving back, affording you the freedom to choose where and how to make a difference. Sometimes life calls you to take a different turn. Don't strike out before you get to first base. Be stalwart and step up to the plate with the faith that God will cast his light toward a new direction with more people, more places, more positivity, and more possibilities.

Turn-taking strategies are made easier when you position yourself in the direction of gratitude and compassion. Embrace silence to regenerate your brain cells, replenish your mental faculties, and tap into your inner stream of emotions, memories, thoughts, and ideas. Meditate and practice mindfulness to bring about equanimity, creativity, and peace. Remain intensely attentive. Be in harmony with that which is needed to create relationships that bear good fruit. Maintain detachment that is devoid of any desired outcome. Focus on what's in front of you and find the self-fulfillment that comes from surrendering control. What will be will be. Sustain a sense of interconnectedness. Power such as you had never imagined will be within your reach.

A wise man will hear, and will increase learning, and a
man of understanding shall attain unto wise counsels.

—Proverbs 1:5 King James Bible

When you *take turns taking the lead*, you allow others to have their time in the winner's circle. You support them in effectively making the shift from child to parent, student to teacher, athlete to coach, employee to entrepreneur, and back again, choosing to alternate who will be in the leadership position. Utilizing this mind-set will allow you time to test the waters and emerge victoriously on the other side.

Turn-taking is a type of organization and discourse that is both verbal and action-oriented. In various contexts, it can be a valuable tool to enhance social, emotional, and cognitive development, which can later translate into more satisfying interpersonal relationships.

Take turns at bat. That alone will gain you a coveted place on the field and access to the game of life with all the frivolity and fierceness it engenders.

While waiting to take your turn, be patient. Put someone else's needs before your own. Forgo the urge for instant gratification. Make a commitment to listen and be wholly and fully present. Be aware of your body language; it speaks volumes. Create a safe space for open dialogue, a judgment/shame-free zone where disparate opinions can be expressed and responded to with empathy and positive regard. Practice these "know and grow" protocols. The shift that occurs will be instrumental in you, consciously creating a better and brighter tomorrow today.

When you take turns taking the lead, your assets outweigh your liabilities, a poignant reminder that the most valuable resource you have is one another.

THE THIRD QUARTER

Midlife (Age 35–53)

Generation X population totals approximately 51 million.

*Somewhere between what you survived, and who
you are becoming is exactly where you're
meant to be. Start loving the journey.*

—J. Raymond

You're in the throngs of midlife, in the midst of a juggling act with adolescents, career, aging parents, financial responsibilities, and extended family and friends, all in dire need of your undivided attention. Your sons and daughters are going off to college or moving out on their own. You're envisioning their journey toward successful adulthood, looking forward to the mature and emotionally meaningful relationships you'll have with them in the future.

Got the spouse and house all to yourself? Check.
Work and family conflicts on the decline? Check.
Are you praying for your sons and daughters? Check.
Trusting God to do what you cannot do? Check.

Breathe a sigh of relief. They're just a phone call, email, text, or video chat away. You've debunked the empty nest syndrome; at least for the time being, let those sublime feelings of joy and pride marinate.

You're in your early forties or fifties, the gold standard in employment, with approximately one-third of your work life still ahead of you. Push the reset button. This could be the perfect time to go back to school, sharpen and renew your skills, make a career change that reflects your present interests, or pursue a goal you were passionate about in the past. In the interim, volunteer or accept a part-time job in your preferred industry. Until you're ready to totally exit the workforce, leverage the power of "bridge" jobs. As you search for vocational satisfaction, free your mind to focus on the growth and abundance to come.

Accelerating to the next level is another exciting option. You've acquired extensive knowledge and stayed linked in over the course of your professional career, been loyal, reliable, and adept at balancing your home/work/life. Those transferable talents along with your years of mentoring and team building can be parlayed into "new, now" opportunities that will challenge and fulfill you. You've done the prep work. Now give yourself time to strategically analyze any career moves you're considering. Make a list of the things you have a heart to do and create a job description that fits those ideals. Determine what gifts you have mastered but have yet to utilize that will make a difference and shift the consciousness of the world.

To stay on point in manifesting your goals, consider creating a vision board; a visible representation of your desires (whatever you want to be, do, or have in your life) placed within your constant awareness. Summon your inner genius. Tap into the feelings this "new normal" will bring; quantify the symbols represented in the pictures and images you select. Add a vision statement to further support your effort. Through the power of your subconscious mind, your highest desires can be brought forth. The investment in time and effort will, no doubt, pay dividends.

On the flip side, you may be parenting your parents (shouldering the responsibility alone or with siblings)—a role reversal that may leave you both struggling with the loss of independence, which can trigger anger, fear, guilt, and depression. Or circumstances may dictate their placement in an assisted-living facility.

Whether they are relatively healthy and independent or contending with an acute condition, elder African Americans prefer to age in place and have a say in their health care—whether allopathic or culturally congruent—which is defined as "cognitively based assistive, supportive, facilitative, or enabling decisions that are tailor-made to fit with the individual's cultural values, beliefs, and life practices." It's a matter of respect (and trust).

The nature of the relationships that exist between dependent elders and their caregivers vary across ethnicity with many African Americans raising children and grandchildren along with caregiving other family members in addition to their elderly parents. They typically provide longer hours and a higher intensity of care with less support, access to services, and fewer resources.

In African American families, caregiving is performed within a collectivistic structure composed of different people with diverse levels of daily involvement. Although most often, one person steps up to the plate and serves in a primary capacity. According to the Caregiving in the US 2015 report, there are 5.6 million African American caregivers, many of whom are middle-aged adult daughters of the care recipients (average age of forty-eight years old). They are far less likely than their Caucasian counterparts to attribute negative mental and health outcomes to their caregiving responsibilities, identifying church and other faith-based organizations as an essential source of social and emotional support—a legacy that's at the heart of our enduring commitment and love.

The Caregivers Bill of Rights, adapted from *Caregiving: Helping an Aging Loved One* by Jo Horne, acknowledges the mental, physical, and emotional challenges caregivers face, offering simple and supportive truths they can reflect on and affirm and a much-needed respite from the stress and strain.

Your marriage may be flourishing or in a state of flux with so-called gray divorce (those aged fifty and older) on the rise, nearly doubling between 1990 and 2010 when it peaked at 25 percent. The United States has the third highest divorce rate in the world, with roughly half of those who were once married living single. Although current research essentially ignores divorce that occurs for those in midlife and older, a notable omission given the US's aging population.

Consider writing the next chapter with your partner by your side. Choose to be in the 50 percent who stay together, creating true happiness and freedom, loving your partner by sharing the love that's within them. Design a durable, supportive, and rewarding template that suits who you are now. You only have to hold up your half. Communication and forgiveness are valuable tools to have in your kit when unconditional love is at the center, serving as the ultimate goal. Be proud. Your relationship hasn't failed or gone out of fashion; it's stood the test of time.

Midlife is a prime time to connect in your relationships, resuscitating those that have been in a coma or lingering on life support. You're more selective in the social and emotional investments you make, so nurture relationships that are comfortable, reliable, and mutually satisfying. Whether old or new, make certain they're built on a love ethic. The countless hours devoted to your career and the kids can now be redirected to create quality time with your significant others.

Hold those who are true to you tenderly with both hands. Designate a date night with your partner. Let it be a special reminder of all the things you love about him/her and why you decided to make that exceptional someone your forever mate. Create individual experiences with your children that are meaningful to them or take a stroll down memory lane with your longtime best friend. Studies have shown that revisiting happy memories from back in the day (or humming a sentimental song) benefits physical, mental, and emotional health as does close friendships, which boosts happiness, strengthens immunity, lowers stress, and improves self-confidence.

Consider expanding your friendship circle, expose yourself to new opportunities and unique perspectives that may push you to venture beyond your comfort zone. It's a positive endeavor—an actionable activity—that will enrich your life immeasurably.

The middle years occur between the age of approximately thirty-five and sixty-four. Like every developmental life stage, the journey taken—whether good, bad, or ugly—is unique (and peculiar) to each individual. The key question to be explored and answered is, Will I provide something of real value? The virtue(s) associated with this life span are *care* and *contemplation,* important social and emotional resources to draw from at any age. This is a new day. A whole new lease on life is awaiting your signature on the dotted line.

It may seem like you have a hundred balls in the air all at the same time—like the Egyptian toss jugglers circa 1990 BC—but there's never been a better time to handle life stressors with finesse. Your experience, heightened intuition, adaptability, and support from your village nurtured over the years has made you, in all things, more than a conqueror equipped to embrace the fullness of life with gratitude and self-confidence.

G. Stanley Hall described middle life as a prime time "when you are at the apex of your aggregate powers," particularly in the areas of leadership within the family, contributions to the community, self-confidence, decision-making abilities, earnings, and professional status with health and well-being of prominent importance. Many experience this as a time for powerful personal growth that can be both beneficial and rewarding. In fact, a substantial percentage of those in the middle years report better-than-ever mental health and self-esteem.

The Upside Downs of Midlife

Metaphorically, midlife is a mirror you gaze into as you reflect on the view of what's been left behind. Sometimes this life span represents the last ditch effort to get it done whatever the *it* happens to be. Conventional wisdom may tell you there's no going back, the past is the past—done, fini, water under the bridge. But when you're still unconsciously dealing with the existential crisis of enslavement, it may be a challenge to reorient yourself to the new identity and possibilities awaiting you on the shore. The insecurity and urgency you may feel during midlife is merely a part of an ever-evolving transition.

In the course of your life, you may have encountered turbulence, waves crashing as you stood in the eye of the storm. Or maybe you're just cruising, smooth sailing through calm waters. Whether you hit rock bottom or sail to safety, lean in like your ancestors did, relying not on your own understanding but God's, and you'll always be lifted. To walk on water, you must first get out of the boat.

For many, feelings of discontent and restlessness emerge in response to new priorities and the need to rewrite past assumptions about life. An African proverb advises, "Don't tear down a fence until you know why it was put up," representing when one fails to see the use of something and seeks to cast it aside before that which is meant to replace it has manifested. No matter the gender, midlife can be an emotionally uncomfortable time, a period of feeling ill at ease as the struggle with aging and mortality ensues, and holding onto a sense of purpose may seem like an impossible dream.[24]

The middle years are all about surrendering to the pull, to forge ahead into uncharted territory, and to having the courage to allow what is being born within to emerge. Prepare yourself by being mindful; connect with deep intention. If a crisis of faith or one of the heart surfaces, check any anxiety you may feel, address the elephant in the room, and dare to mention the unmentionable. Identify what's stirring up your emotions and causing the stress, anger, or sadness

---

[24] Margie E. Lachman, Salom Teshale, and Stefan Agrigoroaei, "Midlife as a Pivotal Period in the Life Course: Balancing Growth and Decline at the Crossroads of Youth and Old Age," *International Journal of Behavioral Development*.

you feel. Don't be overly concerned; most of the changes that will inevitably occur can easily be accommodated.

Minding the Middle

Research confirms that during midlife, the mind not only maintains abilities of youth but acquires new competencies because of the adult brain's capacity to rewire itself. Research suggests, for example, the middle-aged mind is calmer, less neurotic, and better able to sort through social situations with some middle-agers experiencing improved cognitive abilities.

Cognitive neuroscientist Patricia Reuter-Lorenz of the University of Michigan in Ann Arbor alluded to the "enduring potential for plasticity, reorganization, and preservation of capacities during midlife." Comprehensive data on the aging brain were gleaned from the Seattle Longitudinal Study, which has tracked the cognitive abilities of approximately six thousand participants (ages 22–101) over the past fifty-plus years. The results showed evidence that middle-aged adults perform better on four out of six cognitive tests than those same individuals did as young adults.

Verbal and simple math abilities as well as spatial and abstract reasoning skills all improve in middle age. Cognitive skills in the aging brain have also been studied extensively in pilots and air-traffic controllers with older pilots showing overall performance that seemed to remain intact. Researchers tested pilots age forty to sixty-nine as they performed on-flight simulators and found they did a better job than their younger counterparts at achieving their objective. In a study published in *Neurology* on April 2, 2019, researchers found that adhering to Mediterranean diet (MedDiet) patterns and dietary approaches to stop hypertension (DASH) improved midlife cognitive performance. Although additional studies are needed to identify the proper combination of foods and nutrients for optimal brain health across the life span.

The ubiquitous term *midlife crisis* represents the face-to-face encounter with the finitude of life and the pressure of reckoning with the "sands of time" as the years quickly drift away. It's a term coined by psychoanalyst and behavioral scientist Elliott Jaques who studied the careers of artistic geniuses such as Dante and Paul Gauguin, which revealed a pattern of abrupt changes in styles or decline in productivity, which emerged in the middle years. The resulting paper "Death and the Mid-Life Crisis" appeared in the *International Journal of Psychoanalysis* in 1965.

It was a phenomenon alluded to six centuries before in *The Divine Comedy* when the protagonist referred to finding himself lost on a straight path that time had made crooked. According to Jaques, "Dante's descent through Purgatory symbolized both the 'crisis' and its resolution." Although in real-life scenarios, the curves are never quite as dangerous.

The most creative are often plagued with bouts of neuroticism, depression, and obsessional neuroses. In his research, Jaques discovered that many artists either died at midlife—like Mozart, van Gogh, and Chopin—or experienced a powerful transformation that sparked the urge to fully embrace life in all its serious and hard-won expressions. Real-life experiences like those that formed the legacy of John William Coltrane whose musical mastery still looms large nearly fifty-five years after his untimely passing.

The spirit of God emanated from John Coltrane's saxophone; each note an immeasurable equation resonating from the frequency of love. Born September 23, 1923, Coltrane transitioned to the next realm in 1964. His bebop beginnings and hard bop interludes a bridge that continues to transmute psalms of sound, soprano and tenor, which gently course through the cosmos. Coltrane's father, a part-time musician, was his first musical muse. "What I'm becoming," he once said, "my horn will represent."

Through this sacred soundscape, Coltrane grew to the best good possible, soaring higher, deeper, gentler, and sweeter. He recited prayers at the site of Hiroshima with the clouds of dust and charred vapors remnants of the atomic bomb ascending as blessings rained down each note OM a satellite spinning, OM every sunrise, OM an equinox.

A Love Supreme, his magnum opus, was his ode to God, signifying the spiritual awakening that manifested when he was freed from the yoke of drug and alcohol addiction. For Coltrane, the Creator had a master plan.

This beloved son of the Most High created a space for souls to sing. Deeply influenced by religion and spirituality, he intuited the galaxies awaiting and the earth's awakening. Maintaining allegiance to music as moral law that, in the words of Plato, "gives soul to the universe and wings to the mind, allowing our imaginations to take flight."

"My music is the spiritual expression of what I am—my faith, my knowledge, my being . . . When you begin to see the possibilities of music, you desire to do something really good for people, to help humanity free itself from its hang-ups . . . with the realization that good can only bring good."

Unlike Jaques, Erik Erikson understood the risk of reducing creative geniuses to their mental maladies as it fails to explain the mechanisms of their greatness or acknowledge the role their situations may have played in their becoming influencers of such high esteem.

Earlier phases of life and the quality of relationship attachments have important implications as it relates to adjustment, personal satisfaction, and dealing with stress, which can collectively have a far-reaching impact on overall well-being. Periods of turbulence and self-doubt occur across the developmental stages with gained capacity in one dimension often resulting from decline in another.

Such crisis happens less in the middle years and more in young adulthood; it is considered a time of significant turning points.

Mary Lynn Crow's study of women in midlife concluded while many experienced such episodes, those who were successful in that period of transition turned the challenges they faced into opportunities for renewal. In fact, embracing such change lessens the possibility of undergoing this phantom "juncture."

Research challenges the notion that *midlife crisis* is a widespread phenomenon particularly since the term does not appear in either Eastern or African cultures. Although most intense, short-lived, acute, easily identifiable, and defining events can be controlled and managed when we have the dreaded come-to-Jesus chat with ourselves that cracks open our hearts and heals the hurt.

For those of African descent, midlife crisis is a Westernized, societal construct associated with the acceptance of standards set by an ego-driven and materialistic culture that defines a person's worth based on accumulation, accomplishment, and attainment often acquired by any means necessary. When challenge and change is defined in that manner, a scarcity mind-set may surface with the fear of not having (or being) enough, triggering a fight-or-flight response. When you seek balance in the cyclical nature of life, contemplate and recite the book of Ecclesiastes 3:1–8 KJV:

To everything
There is a season
And a time to every purpose under heaven
A time to be born, a time to die
A time to plant, a time to reap
A time to kill, a time to heal
A time to laugh, a time to weep
A time to build up, a time to break down
A time to dance, a time to mourn

To everything
There is a season
And a time to every purpose under heaven

A time to gain, a time to lose
A time to rend, a time to sew
A time for love, a time for hate
A time for peace

I swear it's not too late.[25]

Whether you've endured a life change, have experienced loss, or are in the midst of discovering who you are now, consider directing your energy toward the next optimistic opportunity—the one that moves you from good enough to better, the one that launches you from adequate to extraordinary, the one that gives you the stamina to reach your personal best. For that proverbial eighth time when you rise, dust yourself off *and* shine.

> *Measure success by the lives you change.*
>
> —Casey Gerald, author

Erikson believed that the challenges facing those in midlife—the seventh of his eight psychosocial developmental stages—inspires the broadening of one's concerns and energies as it relates to the welfare of others, which can be positively impactful on a grand scale. This all-encompassing urge to contribute to society for the benefit of future generations represents a main source of balance in this life span.[26]

Erickson referred to this quality as *generativity*, defining it as "the primary task of adult psychosocial development most commonly

---

[25]

[26]   Shawn L. Christiansen and Rob Palkovitz, "Exploring Erikson's Psychosocial Theory of Development: Generativity and Its Relationship to Paternal Identity, Intimacy, and Involvement in Childcare" in *Journal of Men's Studies* (1988).

expressed through parenting." Generativity can be divided into four different theoretical types: biological, parental, technical, and cultural.

Biological generativity refers to what Erikson called procreativity, which author and professor of psychology John Kotre defines as "begetting, bearing, and nursing offspring with the concern being the infant." Biological, social, and psychological clocks dictate changes that occur in all individuals, whether there are similarities in their lifestyles or not. Parental generativity is defined as "nurturing and disciplining offspring and initiating them into family traditions with the object being the child." A generative parent maintains the conviction that his or her efforts are worthwhile contributions toward the development of humankind.

Each generation comes forth ready for the world in which they are birthed with untapped knowledge passed down from one generation to another generation to the next. "Change and become like little children, then you may enter the kingdom of heaven."

Technical generativity involves passing on skills, symbols, and culture to apprentices with cultural generativity, which may peak at different points in the life cycle, centering on both the meaning of the culture's symbol system and passing on the system. It is a two-part process where the person identified as mentor is responsible for holding in balance.[27]

Once an individual has developed a sense of who s/he is (identity) and maintained stable, committed, and loving relationships (intimacy), then s/he is equipped to commit to the next generation (generativity). When coupled with secure attachments, optimism, and openness to diverse experiences, generative concern can promote satisfaction and purpose in life and positively affect life expectancy.

---

[27]   John Kotre, *Make it Count: How to Generate a Legacy that Gives Meaning to Your Life* (The Free Press, 1999).

Many researchers identify generativity as a developmental phase whose contributions to successful aging have yet to be fully acknowledged.

As a result of substantial research, the ideas associated with generativity are now being applied to other stages of the life course, allowing it to be realized through personal, family, or career attainment and achieved through serving in the role(s) of teacher, clergy, and coach or through volunteering, mentoring, and engaging in productive endeavors. Generativity seeks to honor the ability inherent in each of us to create, generate, and produce what is of utmost importance to our world.

Here We Grow Again

Optimally, the middle years open the way for intense and meaningful work that gives birth to creative insight, a sacred undertaking. Writer and philosopher Ayn Rand eloquently described it as "the fullest and most purposeful use of one's mind." The divine exists in the act of creation. Numerous artists, authors, scientists, and psychologists like Carl Jung created some of their best and long-lasting works by (in Jung's case) maintaining a bimodal philosophy, which balances divergent thinking gleaned from periods of extreme isolation and concentration with convergent thinking associated with sorting and analyzing regular day-to-day obligations toward the best outcome. Divergent and convergent thinking are two sides of the same coin, a cognitive process that originates from contrasting rhythms within the brain.

Midlife is a broad topography with definition culled from resurrected thoughts that are reconstructed in a manner that permits new meaning to emerge. Creativity helps us realize our potential—by being alert, questioning, and discovering—so that our own initiative may be awakened. It provides a safe space for self-expression and inquiry as seeded, sprouts of possibility burst through watered by innovative inner knowing. Creativity, manifested in its many diverse ways, can help one navigate a safe journey through the emotional, social, and physical turmoil associated with midlife, serving as a source of well-being in a time of change. Combining elements of a well-lived life with do-it-yourself panache is the epitome of creativity at its best, particularly during midlife. When undertaken authentically, self-absorption (or stagnation) may be transformed into exhilarating self-expression.

Midlife in the United States (MIDUS), the first national study focused on middle-aged adults, investigated the association between health, optimism, positive affect, social support, and the potentially burdensome and stressful life events that can occur during this life span. The broad aim was to identify the biopsychosocial pathways that contribute to diverse health outcomes in the middle years, incorporating factors associated with the normal processes of aging as well as those that are disease-related.

The three major tenets highlighted as particularly relevant in midlife are multidirectionality, variability/plasticity (which research links to greater amounts of physical activity and better brain function), protection/resilience (the capacity to positively adjust to challenging life experiences), and the nature and direction of change that occurs in physical/psychological health and well-being.[28]

Those in midlife play a fundamental role in the lives of individuals on either end of the age spectrum whether at home, in the workplace, or in society at large. Thus, a focus on promoting health and well-being can have a far-reaching impact across multiple generations.

Midlife is presented as a pivotal time of balancing the duality of past/present, growth/decline, strength/weakness, and youth/eldership. Jung described the importance of balancing the different aspects of the self, a process of integrating one's personality that he referred to

---

[28]   Ibid.

as individuation. He saw the middle years as a critical period—the afternoon of life—a nexus between the salutation of the morning and the evening's final dawn.

Welcome to the Second Half

I'm the greatest. I said that even before I knew I was.

—Muhammad Ali,
activist and boxing heavyweight champion

Take a new approach to life; you are what you believe yourself to be. The law of belief affirms that whatever you subconsciously feel to be true in your inner world if thought upon consistently must manifest in your outer world. Your inner thoughts always become your outer reality. Belief is biology especially when it comes to your body. Think greater than you feel. Affirm the power of your own thoughts. Honor your emotions and thought process that emanate from your body and brain, allow it to be your sacred wordbook. Shift your mind-set to positive expectancy. Controlling the quality of your thoughts and feelings allows all the good chemicals and neurotransmitters to flow, which facilitates mental clarity and wisdom. Master this philosophy.

Express your emotions ahead of your experience. Positive emotions and resilience are affirmatively correlated, sharing a bidirectional relationship where one consistently leads to the other. Resilience is significantly related to emotional regulation, allowing certain individuals to bounce back after a tragedy, which can facilitate a stronger sense of life satisfaction. Trust in your future; let go of your past. Fear and courage are two brothers born of the same cloth, as are pain and freedom.

Belief also plays an important role in positive aging. The Centre for Positive Ageing defines it as, "the aspirations of individuals and communities to plan for, approach and live life's changes and challenges as they age and approach the end of their lives, in a productive, active and fulfilling manner. The focus embraces the idea of making the most of opportunities, innovations and research which promote a person's sense of independence, dignity, well-being, good health and enables their participation in society."

Adopt a Daily Spirit/Mind/Body Wellness Regime

Rise and shine; express gratitude for the blessings of this day. There are 86,400 seconds, 1,440 minutes, and 24 hours in a day. Affirm your connection to Source by repeating "I am" statements, which help reduce cortisol levels while simultaneously activating a sense of purpose and inner guidance.

Steady your breath, allow oxygen to feed, and invigorate your brain. Deep, diaphragmatic breathing stimulates the parasympathetic nervous system, allowing blood vessels to open and calming both the heart and nervous system.

Sit quietly and meditate for fifteen minutes. A 2015 study conducted by University of California at Los Angeles found that mindfulness meditation can reduce the negative impact of aging on the brain. Maintaining a state of mindfulness allows one to concentrate fully on a specific thing that is occurring in the present moment, accepting, and nonjudgmentally paying attention to the sensations, thoughts, and emotions that arise. Cultivate a state of mindfulness in your everyday activities, and the mundane will become your muse. In the Buddhist tradition, one focuses on the breath. In Vedic or transcendental meditation, a personal mantra is repeated, while the kindness meditation, a traditional heart practice in Buddhism, readies a kind and caring heart.

Allocate at least twenty to twenty-five minutes to write in your journal; it's a great way to organize your thoughts, dreams, and goals. Or set aside thirty to forty-five minutes to do *Morning Pages,* three pages of longhand, stream-of-consciousness writing done first thing in the morning. This "for your eyes only" morning meditation pokes into the crevices of your consciousness, unleashing your mind to unwind, wander, and ultimately, unearth the thoughts you then place on the pages.[29] It's a clearing exercise that allows you to capture what has ensnared your mind—those cloud thoughts that move through your consciousness—so you can glimpse the higher awareness that is now at your beck and call. Say adios to life as you know it and hola to the existence to come. Write as if your life depends on it. Recording legend stories is the s/hero's journey.

Everyone should consider his/her body as a priceless gift from one whom he loves above all, a marvelous work of art, of indescribable beauty, and mystery beyond human conception, and so delicate that a word, a breath, a look, nay, a thought may injure it.

—Nikola Tesla, inventor, electrical engineer and futurist

Tesla's construct serves as an approach to health and well-being that incorporates a range of esoteric factors. Religion, spirituality, and the capacity to believe in something greater than yourself are of central importance, providing structure and meaning to everyday circumstances as well as support through life's diverse challenges and triumphs.

Pray. It is your intimate time to converse with God. When you pray, your brain goes into its highest state of intellectual functioning. "We are designed to connect with the spirit of God," Christian evangelist Priscilla Shirer said in an interview with neuroscientist Caroline Leaf.

We cannot limit the extraordinary supernatural power of God. Tune in to the needs of others. Ask God what he desires for that person, their families, and communities. Pray in the mind of Christ for the manifestation of their particular needs. Research has shown that when

---

[29]   Julia Cameron, *The Artist's Way: A Spiritual Path to Higher Creativity* (New York: Random House, 1992).

you help others, you increase your own healing by up to 68 percent. Access the power of God; put the laws of love into circulation.

"We have to do the hard work and choose to step into God's love zone, which he has placed in the atmosphere in which we live," Leaf shared. "We are embedded in the ethical values of love. It's a mathematical equation showing the beauty, the logic, and the intelligence of the God we are immersed in when we pray."

Stay emotionally invested in the greatness that is in and of you. Approach any and all signs of success as a duty, obligation, and responsibility that you were born to fulfill. Upgrade your life. Maintain the mind-set that it is a privilege; go out and live it to the fullest.

Be about the Business of You

The middle years are an auspicious time to redefine your life with renewed purpose, commitment, and vision. You only have one life to live, so it's up to you to live it to the max. During midlife, your natural inclination is to encourage and engage others; although equipping yourself with the boldness to examine and question the loss-gain-discovery trifecta takes herculean effort. But you're strong enough, courageous enough, faith-filled enough, and operating from a sustainable God-focused mind. A village of intergenerational stakeholders and allies with mental/spiritual/physical mastery that span the life stages comprise your internal board of directors.

As CEO of "You Inc.," you have taken basic principles of good business and translated them into a teachable course of study that places immense demands on life that without exception must be supplied. Demand that life in all its diversity be abundant; so it is. Demand possession of mental agility and the capacity to reason; so it is. Demand that your body temple function in optimal health; so it is. Demand that your family, community, and country be protected and prospered; so it is. Demand that your purpose in life evolve and that it be made manifest; so it is. Demand that the power and presence of God be within you; so it is. Make your demands, and the Most High will create the supply. Life will not make any arbitrary demands of you when you first unapologetically make the desires of your heart known. Proactivity—not chance—determines what each second, moment, hour, and day will bring.

You are your only competition and have earned the right to stand behind who you are with pride. You've taken the high road on your way up and, with confidence, implemented change where needed, always leaving room for improvement. Helping others in pursuit of their life mission has consistently upped your game. As the source of the inspiration, you seek to set in place; you must consistently refocus and realign your efforts so key priorities are obtained. Take note of your attitude and aptitude and remember you (the alchemist) are both the question and the answer—everything that is is already within you. Spend your time and expend your energy like a prospérer. Be about the business of you. Refuel every day, hold an intention that translates into a goal that magnifies a greater expression of *you*, the human territory God has given you to have sovereignty over for a "season, a reason, and a lifetime."

Say What You Mean and Mean What You Say

From the 'hood to the Amen corner, our word has always been our bond. You can find references to its biblical origins in Numbers 30:2, when the Hebrew elder Moshe instructs the tribes of Israel, "When a man . . . swears an oath to bind his soul with a *bond*, he shall not break his *word*; he shall do according to all that proceeds out of his mouth." (R. A. Torrey, *The Treasury of Scripture Knowledge*)

You travel light when your words are your bond. When you honor the special significance of keeping your word, it's easy to find what you're looking for. No heavy baggage to weigh you down or hidden agendas with half-truths tucked in every situation. When your word is your bond, you're free to say what's on your mind. You cannot speak for your partner, your children, your family, your community, your culture, or your country. You can only speak for yourself. When you do that, saying what you mean and meaning what you say is the natural order of things.

During slavery, our words were weaponized, so we held our tongues as a form of bonding, a promissory note that vouched for our willingness to be all in for our sisters and brothers. Telling our truth was an act of treason, a disloyal behavior often punishable by law. As a result, we learned to practice dissimulation—tricking, fooling, bamboozling, and deceiving one another—when all we want in our hearts of hearts is open and honest communication that creates positive, loving, and long-lasting relationships. The practice of falsehood continues, and truth-telling remains a rarity, with our very presence revealing the lies that still linger and trigger intergenerational trauma and pain.

Keeping feelings bottled up may cause you to blow your top. Instead of going to great lengths to keep your composure, let your guard down. Express your emotions, whether positive or negative, it's crucial to your mental health. Sharing your authentic feelings and working through your issues with others is the only approach to take. Spend some quality time listening. Often, the perspective that your loved ones share (and those you've falsely demonized) may pleasantly surprise you.

Speaking truth to power isn't about saying politically incorrect things that make those in authority cringe. It's a nonviolent, political tactic employed to create a more just and truthful world and the peace that must manifest itself in everything we do. Say what you mean and have the audacity to feel good about it. Then everyone's freed up to be their more unique and authentic selves.

Maintain a Sense of Purpose

Wanna change the world? Or is it sufficient to find new meaning in your day-to-day existence? Either way, bigging up your sense of purpose is a great first step. Discipline correlates to purpose, and maintaining a sense of purpose in your life is integral to staying happy and healthy.

Living a purposeful life improves longevity, lowering the risk of disease, and heightening overall well-being. Among older adults, it plays a significant role in maintaining physical function. Increase your sense of purpose by being a helpmate to others, choosing a hobby and/or cultivating relationships.

Set new goals and develop new habits whether it's starting a community garden, learning a new language, volunteering at a local homeless shelter, or even launching a new career. Aging, retirement, and other challenges associated with this life span can easily be offset when there is structure in your life. Renew your priorities and motivation, add that to the mix, and the fear of mortality substantially decreases with reductions in heart failure and Alzheimer's disease.

Our beloved ancestors maintained their sense of purpose by keeping the culture alive, retaining their indigenous identity, and making European forms serve African functions. They leaned in, drawing insight from their heritage of ancient wisdom and knowing and combining Eurocentric belief systems with Mother Africa's moral and spiritual divine law. Our ancestors remain the source of life for us, their living descendants, whom they bequeathed with ancient wisdom that sustains us to this day.

Think about Your Legacy

A good man leaves an inheritance to his children's children.

—Proverbs 13:22 (New American Standard Bible),
words Solomon spoke to his son in

As a parent and/or grandparent, you are of a certain age when you will soon pass on the greatest inheritance known to man—wisdom, love, encouragement, memories, and lessons learned—what the Heavenly Father and your foreparents left the world.

The middle years are a time to consider your legacy and the influences you've had on the world around you. If life hasn't been everything you thought it should be, start making changes now. If it has, celebrate, take the time to smell the roses, and keep it moving.

Scrutinize your values and priorities; make certain they align with your behavior and conduct. Rewrite your life history, and be the architect of a new blueprint. Take the journey within and record it for posterity. How you see yourself reflects how others see you. If you've been looking at your life through the lens of a painful, traumatic past, go deeper and find the love that sustained its humble beginnings. What will you be known for when you leave this realm? The moral of this story is you always get to choose.

Nighttime Is the Right Time to Catch Some Zzzs

If you think that when you snooze, you lose, you're wrong. In fact, good sleep habits promote everything from memory to sound mental health to hormone regulation and increases the body's ability to heal. It's a natural rejuvenator.

According to the CDC, adults in midlife should get seven to eight hours of sleep. Approximately thirty million people are affected by chronic insomnia, although a lack of sleep need not take a toll on your well-being. If you're having problems counting sheep, start by maintaining a consistent bedtime, which can positively impact your mood, lower stress, increase energy levels, and positively affect your ability to function optimally throughout the day. Create a power-down, before-bed routine that sends a mental signal that it's time for rest and relaxation. This can be attributed to the hormone melatonin, which is naturally secreted in the brain when the sun goes down. When sleep is disrupted, hormone levels are cut off, which can trigger headaches. Read a book, listen to relaxing music, take a warm bath, or do yoga or stretching exercises. Turn off the television and all technology; blue light generated by electronic devices can delay the onset of sleep. Spending one additional minute on your phone can rob you of one hour of slumber. If necessary, explore other self-care options that enable you to get additional rest. Before you crawl under the covers, visualize yourself sleeping peacefully through the night and waking in the morning reinvigorated, ready to have a winning day.

Is It Hot in Here, or Is It Just Me?

Menopause can be the most enlightening, satisfying, and freeing time of a woman's life—a period of personal empowerment with the emergence of wisdom, strength, and mental/physical/spiritual well-being. In that sense, the change becomes a type of currency when women find value in the feminine odyssey and the divine energy that transmutes across the life stages—from puberty, adolescence, early adulthood to the exalted state of wise womb. According to Chinese and Ayurvedic medicine, age sixty marks the time when a woman begins to develop her soul. What she creates for herself that benefits the people around her is the primary focus.

Menopause is defined as "the cessation of menstruation," which typically occurs around the age of fifty-one after a woman has missed twelve periods consecutively. Perimenopause can occur four or more years prior to its onset. Menopause is a process that involves the whole woman's mind, body, and spirit and is inclusive of all its aspects.

Coupled with midlife, menopause can be both acute and challenging with a plethora of symptoms, which include hot flashes (affecting the hypothalamus, the area of the brain that regulates body temperature), weight gain, and vaginal dryness all caused by decreased production of estrogen and progesterone accompanied by chemical changes that trigger a myriad of psychological responses.

In her book, *The Wisdom of Menopause*, Christiane Northrup, MD, champions the change as so much more than a random collection of symptoms that need to be "repaired," viewing it instead as a multidimensional revolution that brings about the most expansive growth since adolescence. The variations are unlimited.

Anthropologist Margaret Mead, who undertook her most prolific work while in her sixties and seventies, coined the term *postmenopausal zest* (PMZ) in the 1950s, defining it as a "psychological and physiological surge of energy" that sparks increased creativity and drive that is long-lasting.

A British Psychological Society study found that most women felt better at sixty than they did at forty with improvement in cognitive function and memory. The choices a woman makes have the power to secure vibrant health and well-being for the remainder of her life.

Culture plays an important role in the way black women feel and respond to the change when it occurs. Their preferred sources of information about menopause and the shift in the reproductive system typically come from their mothers, with respect given to other elder women in their communities.

Culture and life events inform the ways in which menopausal symptoms are managed with a high percentage of black women preferring to utilize noninvasive treatments like change of diet, exercise, alternative complementary therapies, prayer, and spirituality. On the plus side, black women are less likely than any other ethnic group to experience somatic symptoms such as headaches, sleeping problems, increased heart rate, and stiffness and soreness in the joints.

If menopause is rocking the boat, don't go overboard. Your mothers and grandmothers made it through; trust and believe that so will you.

Andropause (male menopause) is a collection of symptoms, including fatigue and a decrease in libido, experienced by some middle-aged men that is typically attributed to a gradual decline in testosterone levels that may drop 1 percent per year. Andropause generally occurs when a man reaches age forty. Although symptoms vary, the most common ones include decreased sexual performance, erectile dysfunction, chronic fatigue, sleep disturbances, mood changes, increased irritability, anger, depression, loss of muscle mass, and increased body fat.

Consider incorporating the following natural remedies and implementing lifestyle changes that alleviate or treat any symptoms you may be experiencing. Increase your consumption of omega-3 rich foods. Take supplements—to raise testosterone levels or reduce estrogen levels—that have demonstrated effectiveness, such as broccoli sprout extract, cayenne, green tea extract, magnolia tree bark, muscadine grape skin, mushrooms, omega-3 fatty acids (e.g., fish oil, krill oil), pomegranate, quercetin, resveratrol, turmeric, vitamin D, and zinc. Eat your fruits and veggies; they have high levels of antioxidants, polyphenols, vitamins, minerals, and fiber. Stay hydrated; it's good for the body and assists in releasing toxins. Choose natural therapies such as acupuncture, biofeedback, hormone restoration, and stress management techniques—all of which can lessen symptoms. Avoid supplements, additives, and nutrients that are harmful to overall health, including but not limited to meat, dairy, and foods high in sugar. But first, consult a knowledgeable health-care professional you can trust.

No, Lucille, the Thrill Isn't Gone

Midlife can be a wild and raucous ride that reignites sexual energy. While the frequency may decline, there's a blessed assurance that you and your partner can turn the intimacy up a notch or two well into late adulthood. A survey published in *The New England Journal of Medicine* showed that those referred to as the middle-old age, seventy-five to eighty-four, still nurture intimate relations with more than 20 percent reporting time set aside at least once a week for sexual healing.

Ladies, are you worried about sexual function? Strengthen the pelvic floor with Kegel exercises. Boost your sex drive, increase body awareness, and blood flow to the genital area and rid the body of toxins through yoga. Sexual activity helps the vagina maintain tone and lubrication. Physical affection and engaging in kissing and cuddling strengthens both the emotional and physical bond.

Enjoy prolonged foreplay; explore sex toys together. Try a little intimate touch, massage, and kissing to maintain amour. Sharing your fantasies with your partner can be a huge turn on. Put all anxiety on pause. Be natural; leave performing to the actors. Sex is beneficial to your body, mind, and spirit. And like a fine wine, it just gets better with time.

It's the Pleasure Principle

The vagina (or *yoni*, a Sanskrit word meaning "gift of life," symbolizing divine, procreative energy) possesses protective abilities and glands that release fluids that are designed to stimulate its self-cleansing properties. Its taut muscle tissue has amazing elasticity to accommodate penises of all shapes and dimensions and expand enough for a baby to pass through. The vagina is malleable, able to change in size and shape during arousal. Research indicates that the clitoris (located where the inner labia meet) has eight thousand nerve endings—the highest concentration in the entire human body—while the penis has a mere four thousand.

To enhance your health below the belt, incorporate these vagina-friendly foods into your daily menu. For urinary tract health, drink cranberry juice. Eat more sweet potatoes and probiotic-rich (lactofermented) foods like kimchi, yogurt, sauerkraut, and pickled cucumbers. They are the key to boosting good bacteria, which in turn colonizes the vagina and warding off infections. Oily fish, walnuts, and eggs contain omega-3 fatty acid that increase circulation and sex drive. Apples are in the *When Sally Met Harry* "I'll have what she's having" category. The phloridzin found in these delicious red honeycrisps is said to promote better sexual function, arousal, and lubrication and increase the ability to orgasm. The rich, libido-boosting properties in avocados strengthen vaginal walls and enhance estrogen levels, while leafy greens decrease vaginal dryness. For optimum affect, avoid all white sugar, trans fats, and processed foods.

Don't limit your access; take a hands-on approach. Let your fingers do the walking by exploring your vagina's anatomy. Tender loving care goes a long way. When you get to know your honeypot, you'll never underestimate your supernatural powers again.

A Little (More) Food for Thought

Pomegranates are a natural aphrodisiac that have been associated with fertility and abundance for centuries. Consumption of pure pomegranate juice significantly increases salivary testosterone levels, which can lead to heightened moods and increased sexual drive. If you're concerned with erectile dysfunction, "you can't lose with what you use" since pomegranate juice is a natural remedy for impotence. Zinc assists in the production of men's sex hormones and boosts libido. Oysters, crabs, lobsters, nuts, beans, and whole grains are just a sample of the mineral-rich foods that can turn up the heat. Your sexual satisfaction will skyrocket.

INTRODUCTION TO THE FOURTH QUARTER

Pitch In and Be a Catcher

He who masters the power formed by a group
of people working together has within his grasp
one of the greatest powers known to man.

—Idowu Koyenikan, author of
Wealth for All: Living a Life of Success
at the Edge of Your Ability

All manner of riches are accessible when you do your due diligence. Sometimes you trip. But stumbling is not falling, so you need not question your ability to rise and dare greatly. Remember all the pulling together, lending a hand, participating, cooperating, and contributing because those were the work that earned you this opportunity to discover who you are—an essential aspect of a mystical, magical grand design.

When you pitch in, you get all the glory, but when you're there to catch those who've temporarily lost their footing, it can be a heavy load. Having someone witness your missteps can be embarrassing to the ego that will wage war in its fight to be right even at the expense of severing relationships that could foster the authenticity and compassion you so desire. You came forth to live your own life and, if need be, suffer the consequences until you remember that only you can save yourself. It is in those times of challenge and change when your true character is revealed.

"Fall down seven times, get up eight" reflects the power of resilience and cooperative collaboration. Bear down and put your shoulder to the wheel. Be diligent; never give up.

Catchers are selfless; they know it's not about them. They can't let anything pass them by. Instead they dive, leap, collide, and risk sustaining the bumps and bruises that come with the territory, winding up and controlling their reaction to life's curve balls with gratitude. They are often the overcomers who embody their own definitions of bravery, donning their inner armor and propelling themselves to the core of their greatness for it is at that very edge where the world they dreamed for themselves and others lies.

Operate from your opponents' strengths, not his or her weaknesses. Be inspired to reach higher. Focus on the team, not on the attack. Visualize all the home runs that are just a pitch away. Ready yourself to master the game within the game. Avoid engaging in diversion and amusement. Move beyond the illusion. Do it for the coming generations.

THE FOURTH QUARTER

Late Adulthood (Age 53–70)

Baby boomers' population totals 74 million.

*The hard thing when you get old is to keep your horizons
open. The first part of your everything is in front of you, all
your potential and promise. But over the years, you make
decisions; you carve yourself into a given shape. Then the
challenge is to keep discovering the green growing edge.*

—Dr. Howard Thurman, author,
educator, lecturer, philosopher, and public theologian

Late adulthood need not find you inextricably bound, restricting
yourself to life's outer perimeters. Immersed in the "would have,"
"should have," and "could have" beens; modals of lost opportunity
that define present feelings about past situations. Put a pin in
bitterness, depression, and despair. Know that a continent of dreams
still awaits fulfillment.

You are an elder, a respected member of your family and community,
sheltered in life's upward grasp. You have blossomed and grown
through many life stages from infancy, puberty, adolescence, early
adulthood, midlife, and are now in late adulthood, which spans from
approximately age sixty-five to the end of life. Many African cultures
assign elder status to those age fifty and up.

The key question to be explored and answered is, Have I lived a full
life? The virtue associated with this life span is *wisdom*—experience
and knowledge acquired over the years—and the acceptance of life in
the face of dying and death, a destination we all share. In the words

of author and monk Thomas Merton, this is a time to "detach from yourself in order to see and use all things in and for God."

Embrace the Art of Aging

Maximize your remaining time on earth. Carve out living space that suits you. Follow your heart and intuition. "We are alive," offers creative/influencer Gilbert Everald Young, "flowing like a riveting body of water creating a kind of friction that allows us to comprehend the rhythms of life."

> I am a seventy-year-old artist and have nurtured my craft since the age of six. I surround myself with only that which is conscious and supreme. Everything in the universe is ordered—it is the nature of Maat; the personification of truth and justice with all things bound together in an indestructible unity.

> I knew I had a unique talent, a gift. After high school, I traveled to Europe. I dreamed about going before the opportunity occurred. I had already studied the masters so seeing their work right in front of my eyes amazed me as did the realization that I, too, would create something of immense value. It was as if I had been reincarnated.

> There is a rhythm to what I do as an artist. Music is an integral part of my creation process. Like a verse or chorus from a song, my ideas and tempo may change, but I always start from a solid foundation that is specifically focused. Being an artist allows me the liberty of self-awareness; a consciousness of myself as a hue-man of African descent. Our history goes back eons; before Caucasians came, we were here.

Everything in the universe is scientifically based. Within blackness exists that which is most total and complete; that is the essence of the night. You can see everything—in its entirety . . . it is infinity. Without blackness, only nothingness exists. There is no greater gift than to know what's been hidden from you and to realize that nothing is ever lost. However, that discovery process requires self-inventory.

I am free and maintain a deep awareness of my own freedom. I am highly emotional and have found a way to harness that energy through my art. I always wanted to be myself, following my own lead and embarking on my own journey. I never want to be led by others like a sheep. I make adjustments to accommodate my own ideas and ideals. I know the truth and comprehend exactly what I am sensing and saying. I see who I really am and experience joy by what is reflected back to me.

I am happy with who I am; always grateful for the sound guidance my ancestors provide. I want people to know, "I AM." I wouldn't trade what I've become for anything in this world and neither should you.

Find your niche; always strive to be yourself. Avoid being fearful. Stand on your own ground. Everything must be earned. Use others only to discover where (and how far) you can go."

Erik Erikson defined late adulthood as an optimal time to discover meaning in life (which Gilbert Young alludes to) that arouses a sense of satisfaction and pride in accomplishments earned and the ability to recollect and reminisce about the past with minimal regrets. It is a period of introspection that is most productive when experienced in the presence of significant others. Fulfilling one's inheritance is a primary task in this life span with integrity and despair functioning as alternating states of being that must remain balanced.

The brain continues creating new neurons throughout the life span, an aspect of development that is unique to humankind. New neurons in the hippocampus (involved in regulating memory and emotional response to stress) perform a crucial role in the integration of complex information, which can be transmitted to future generations according to Maura Boldrini, MD, PhD, associate professor of neurobiology at Columbia University and lead author of a study published in the journal *Cell Stem Cell* and who showed that neurogenesis—the process by which neurons or nerve cells are generated in the brain—continues as we age. With a healthy lifestyle, social/intellectual interactions, and exercise, the functioning of those neurons can sustain health and wholeness for years to come.

During late adulthood, aging expresses itself in outward appearance, which is indicative of primary aging (gradual, time-related biological processes seen as universal, i.e., decline in heart, lung, kidney, and muscle function) and pathological/secondary aging (resulting from a particular condition or illness). Both of which counterbalance the understanding, patience, experience, and wisdom aging brings— qualities that profoundly improve life despite changes that may occur. Our ancient African kinship systems and the web of relationships threaded by family and community are the basis of this life span's emotional, social, and cognitive cohesion. Research has shown that family provides identity, support, and social integration throughout life. Resiliency, powerful family ties, and religious values are often nurtured and preserved by the elders.

Aging is a process that is both biological and cultural, a miraculous thing of intense beauty meant to be savored. But how do you live elderhood to the fullest in a culture where youth is fetishized? Other questions come to mind when thoughts about identity and one's relationship in and to the world emerge. What do I truly want to do? How can I make these years the best they can be? Inquiring minds want to know. Erikson argued that the Western fear of aging keeps us from living full lives and further noted, "Lacking a culturally viable ideal of old age, our civilization does not really harbor a concept of the whole of life."

There are as many paths on this life journey as there are human beings in existence. Show what you know. Institute your own "genius hour" (also referred to as 20 percent time or passion time). See the purpose in your life and sense its everlasting value. Set aside sixty minutes to develop new skills or work on a passion project. Live every day as if it were a fresh new start. Set your life commandments, the principles, and beliefs you intend to live by in place. Identify diverse nuggets of thought that will nourish your spiritual, intellectual, and physical yearnings. You get to choose which door(s) to open; you alone hold the key.

Rise to your eldership, contemplating with deep intention the viable substantive life you could be living now. Be mindful of the moment-to-moment, day-to-day reality that will inform your future legacy. Hold yourself accountable for the consequences of your actions, past and present. Create a space for intergenerational dialogue and collaboration—a virtual think tank—where issues of importance to your community and nation are collectively addressed. Generations across the life span will experience the impact of positive change when the mistakes and missteps of the past are acknowledged and forgiven.

Many cultures celebrate the aging process, honoring old age and venerating its elders. Elderhood is identified with wisdom and a close proximity to God. Much of the Korean regard for aging is rooted in the Confucian principle of filial piety, one of the highest moral values pertaining to the respect of one's parents and the deference shown to older individuals and authority figures, a startling contrast to the ageism that occurs in American culture and the stereotypes that silence and devalue the lived experiences of older adults.

In Native American culture, tribal elders are the repositories and transmitters of cultural and philosophical knowledge. Bound by the Creator and his creations, these designated wisdom keepers are essential to the maintenance of life and thus placed at its center. The power and love they carry in their DNA serves as a divine connection to ancestors like Sitting Bull, a Hunkpapa Lakota and holy man who wrote, "I am a red man. If the Great Spirit had desired me to be white, he would have made me so in the first place. He put in your heart certain wishes and plans, and in my heart, he put other and different desires. Each man is good in his sight. It is not necessary for eagles to be crows."

The high status of older people in African cultures is synonymous with the idea that family growth is fortuitous, a source of security in times of crisis, leaving behind descendants who will honor those elders as they move into the ancestral realm. It is a position of authority typically assigned to older men although communities exist where women reject this imposed subordinate status.

The honor afforded elders often corresponds to their ability to control information, property, and resources particularly when they display knowledge, diplomacy, and social connections—skills which are considered community assets.

Numerous African societies were governed by elders (gerontocracy) for the greater good of the community based on the concept of *ubuntu*, a Nguni Bantu term meaning "humanity." Author and professor George Jerry Sefa Dei defines *gerontocracy* as "the traditional African respect for the authority of elderly persons for their wisdom, knowledge of community affairs, and 'closeness to the ancestors.'"

The Bible references the special position within the family held by the elders as revealed in the works of Jethro, a godly man of great integrity. He was Moses' African father-in-law who extended his support to Moses and equipped him for more purposeful and effective leadership. Jethro helped Moses recognize his own need for community in leading God's people, advising him to form a council of elders, "able men from all the people, men who feared God, men who were trustworthy, and placed such men over the people as chiefs of thousands, of hundreds, of fifties, and of tens," (Exodus 18:21 ESV)—men of godly stature who share similarities with those who have strengthened and bound together African societies since the beginning of time.

Elderhood: Building a Sustainable Community

Most black neighborhoods have "community of other mothers and fathers (a council of elders)" whose collective and accumulative wisdom empowers them to provide conscious and intentional analysis, critiques, and solutions to the everyday conditions and situations that affect the places and spaces where people gather and live.

Like many elder activists who stood at the vanguard, Lee Faye Mack (affectionately known as Mother Mack) utilized political and social agitation through militant action, enacting change that would meet the needs of the black community of which she was an integral part. Mother Mack was a major catalyst in the development of the Winston-Salem Black Panther Party, the first Southern chapter formed in 1969 during a volatile time of social and political upheaval. It was a plan of action Rev. Dr. Cheryl Townsend Gilkes refers to as "going up for the oppressed" to secure "a type of economic and career mobility comprised of a set of activities aimed at the empowerment of the powerless."

Community of other mothers and fathers may also take the form of a beloved teacher or a benefactor like Sylvia Bloom, a ninety-six-year-old former legal secretary who bequeathed the bulk of her nine-million-dollar fortune to the Henry Street Settlement, which has opened doors to opportunity to disadvantaged students over the course of its 126-year history.

Such kinship networks, the system of formal and informal relationships that make up an extended family are a mainstay in working class, religious, and immigrant communities and are central to the experience of African Americans a form of parenting that continues to this day. The fluidity of the black family can be traced back to the time of enslavement when every member of the community was expected to look out for every child so none could ever be left behind.

It is the elders, God's hands and heart, whom he promises to take care of as seen in the book of Ruth. God assured Naomi that she would have someone close by her side, and he chose Ruth who committed to caregiving her with loving-kindness. And God, in turn, committed to enabling (and prospering) Ruth.

He affirmed the productivity in old age, stating, "The righteous will flourish like a palm tree. They will still bear fruit in old age, they will stay fresh and green, proclaiming, 'The Lord is upright; he is my Rock,'" (Psalm 92:12–15 New International Version).

The elders who comprise the council may be consulted on a variety of matters pertaining to family and business disputes and social activities/projects while maintaining responsibility for reinforcing rules and regulations. The guidelines for choosing council members vary from community to community.

Whether it takes the shape of a grassroots organization, neighborhood, or civic engagement association, the presence of caring, concerned elders or other mothers and fathers invokes reverential feelings that affirm their importance as the pinnacle of society and trusted keepers of our inheritance.

Although late adulthood can hold a number of existential challenges, when the "weight of the world" is lifted, those in this life span are freed to provide inspired experiences shared with community, friends, and family for the edification of God and everyone involved.

Grandparenting with a Purpose

Many in late adulthood discover new roles to play that reignite their experience and wisdom. One common family occurrence that takes place during middle and late adulthood involves becoming a grandparent, a role that can often inspire a renewal of the parent/adult-child relationship.

African American families have historically been horizontal in structure, with fewer years between generations and more members in each. This horizontal structure often results in juggling the demands of caring for children *and* aging parents. An issue of particular relevance for African American female daughters who are usually the primary caregivers. But there's no need for dismay. Just look closer, you'll see the silver lining surrounding the cloud.

In the book *Grandmother's at Work: Juggling Families and Jobs*, sociologist Madonna Harrington Meyer examined the stories of forty-eight grandmothers who worked while rearing their grandchildren, among the 46 percent in the US who pick up the slack by providing childcare. These are grandmothers, like Marian Shields Robinson (Michelle Obama's mother), who stepped in to share child-rearing duties for the first family's eight-year stay.

In traditional African cultures, grandparents form an important element of the extended family with clearly delineated roles in relation to the care and nurturing of children. Grandparents exercise their authority on matters related to the family with descendants expected to be obedient to the seniors' directives.

Grandmothers are a source of information, wisdom, and comfort for members of the community who generally find consolation and confidence in seeking their advice, which is generally received with great regard. For many, they are the pot of gold at the end of the rainbow.

Societies across the globe acknowledge the influential role grandmothers play in the socialization, acculturation, and care of children as they grow and develop and in the education and supervision of their daughters and daughters-in-law.

Scientists believe grandmothers were crucial to human evolution. As they assumed more child-rearing responsibilities, more offspring could be produced at shorter intervals, helping to pass the longevity gene on to future descendants who had longer adult life spans as a result—a phenomena referred to as the grandmother effect.[30]

Kristen Hawkes, professor of anthropology at the University of Utah, references the grandmother effect in the research that she and James O'Connell conducted in the 1980s, asserting that "grandmothering was the initial step toward making us who we are."

This hypothesis stemmed from their observations of northern Tanzania's Hadza people whose elder women maintain food-gathering practices, spending four to six hours a day foraging tubers, baobab fruit, berries, and other edibles, which are correlated with the nutritional well-being of their grandchildren. Genetic testing confirmed that the Hadza represent one of the primary roots of the human family tree, perhaps more than one hundred thousand years old, although they don't keep close track of years or units of time. Given the wide-ranging role grandmother's play, they should be viewed as key proponents in the advancement of the people.

---

[30] Lindsay Abrams, "The Evolutionary Importance of Grandmothers" in *The Atlantic*, October 24, 2012.

The Emergence of the Grandfamily

As of 2017, 2.8 million young people—about 4 percent of American children—were being raised by 2.6 million grandparents, according to the US Census Bureau. Nationally, the number of children raised by their grandparents increased by nearly 15 percent between 2007 and 2017.

More than half of grandparents raising their children's children are among the working poor, barely meeting the demands of low-paying jobs with one in five living below the poverty line—$24,250 for a family of four. One-third of grandfamilies have grandfathers as the head of the household. Many are battling acute illness, with one-fourth of those grandparents caring for children while on disability.

With family members to raise them, these children have permanent and stable homes and are empowered to maintain connections to siblings and ties to their community and cultural heritage. Despite the obstacles, grandfamilies can make it through the mental and physical ordeals whole. It takes courage, unconditional love, and the belief that through tenacity and sheer will, they are destined to face (and overcome) the complexities of the future—together.

Aging with Intention

Japan has the highest population of elderly with one in five age seventy or older.[31] Over thirty thousand centenarians celebrate their one hundredth birthdays annually. Although Japanese elders face the same challenges associated with aging worldwide, the approach they take is often influenced by their life purpose and determined by their *ikigai* (i-ka-guy), which combines the symbols that define "life" with "to be worthwhile."

---

[31] Justin McCurry, "Japanese Centenarian Populations Edges Towards 70,000" in *The Guardian*, September 14, 2018.

This art of living a full life is about spending your days feeling authentically connected to what is meaningful, brings happiness, and offers a reason to rise and meet the day with supreme focus and joy. Ikigai guides elders' daily practices, and because it's approached with positivity and intentionality, it inspires productivity and active engagement with family, friends, and society.

To discover, pursue, and nurture your ikigai require patience and the ability to relax into the deep dive within that is required. Being in alignment with your ikigai heightens the sense of identity and social value, which is crucial to successful aging. To be in pursuit of personal passion and the life-giving energy it brings no matter the rhyme or reason is the most auspicious end result.

Ikigai finds its strength in the following rules: stay active (don't retire), take it slow (enjoy life more), do not fill your stomach (be disciplined in your habits), surround yourself with friends you trust, smile, reconnect with nature, give thanks, and live in the moment. Always follow your personal ikigai by identifying these: what you love, what you are good at, and the medium through which you can express (and be compensated) for your passion.[32]

A Search for Contentment

Psychiatrist Robert Butler introduced the concept of life review as a developmental task associated with assessing and making sense of one's life. He theorized that those in late adulthood are typically in search of personal meaning, preoccupied with achievements and the ultimate religious or spiritual questions that arise when such internal inquiry and mental processing occurs. Life review is considered a customary activity that assists one in outlining memories and lived experiences for the benefit of family, friends, and other loved ones. Many in this life span find ways to reintegrate long neglected aspects

[32]   Héctor García and Francesc Miralles, *Ikigai: The Japanese Secret to a Long and Happy Life* (Penguin Books, 2016).

of their identity and, in the process, manifest the positive potential it offers in the remaining years of life.

A life review can result in diverse outcomes ranging from depression caused by loneliness and the loss of significant relationships, despair or acceptance, and satisfaction. Reframing past experiences and unsettled conflicts through the lens of personal wisdom can positively affect cognitive functioning. When a life review is seen in a positive light, the individual develops inner peace and the capacity to forgive.

One's ability to tease out recollections of early life events and reweave disparate elements of identity into some form of a coherent whole offers its own reward. Erikson theorized that wisdom symbolized the key strength that emerges from an optimal resolution in the struggle for integrity and integration, which has been the subject of much empirical study related to successful life in the later years. Although the dynamics associated with the art of living differ significantly for each individual—it is a universal principle.

The 4-1-1 of Successful Aging

One model of successful aging developed in 1998 by John Wallis Rowe, MD, and Robert L. Kahn defined it as the "absence of disease, disability, and risk factors, maintaining physical and mental functioning and active engagement with life."

According to a study published in the *Journal of Gerontology: Social Sciences,* Rowe and Kahn's theory may be better characterized as individual resources—unequally distributed across the life span — that are in service to outcomes, which are conditioned by social structure and environment.

It is a departure from the original Rowe and Kahn model, which asserts that preventative strategies can maximize successful aging. Primary, secondary, tertiary, and quaternary prevention models occur respectively: prior to the existence of the disease condition, after the diagnosis but before significant change occurs, and as a means to manage pain and avoid secondary chronic conditions so that functional capabilities for those living with long-term illnesses are improved. In this scenario, disease prevention and health promotion go hand in hand.

Rowe and Kahn's conceptualization on successful aging is prolific. However, many have criticized the model because of its singular focus on late adulthood, a static assessment given the fact that this developmental process occurs over the life course and is not specific to one life stage. Understanding and managing the needs of those in late adulthood over time may offer the opportunity to refine the definition(s) associated with successful aging.

Emotional independence, the ability to exercise greater control, and willpower over our internal states can also lead to successful aging. The opposite of which "situational happiness" can cause immeasurable suffering with its focus on external (and conditional) circumstances that rarely ever bring sustainable joy and well-being.

And be not conformed to this world: but be ye transformed by the renewing of the mind that ye shall prove what is that good, and acceptable, and perfect, will of God.

—Romans 12:2 King James Version

Spirituality, religion, and belief have a dynamic impact on aging, particularly for those in late adulthood, providing the structure, meaning, and understanding needed to face life's triumphs and tribulations. The sense of purpose, transcendence of self, and an internalized relationship with the sacred facilitate a deeply personal odyssey offering a lens through which one may interpret, understand, evaluate, and respond to the complexities and diverse possibilities inherent in our living world.

The story of Job, "a perfect and upright man," and the tragedy that tested his faith hallmark a believer's ability to cultivate a viable response to physical and psychological stress. Recent increases in neuroscientific knowledge and usage of functional magnetic resonance imaging (fMRI) techniques offer a glimpse into the neurophysiological coping mechanisms associated with worship and prayer, which makes Job's response, the "Christian thing to do," appropriate for the grief he was experiencing.

Christ Jesus spoke the words of John 16:33 King James Bible recalling stories of the Bible and the believers who "searched scriptures daily" and devoted to spend twelve minutes in the presence of the Lord, "These things I have spoken unto you, that in me ye might have peace. In the world ye shall have tribulation: but be of good cheer I have overcome the world."

"Dopamine is an important neurotransmitter in the central nervous system shown to be highly active in important executive functions like motor control, cognition, memory creation, and reward-directed behavior. It's also a chemical precursor important in the fight-or-flight reaction."[33] The long-term effects associated with primordial response can increase cardiovascular risk, stroke, diabetes mellitus, and a host of other disorders. The hyperventilation of the amygdala and subsequent volume increase has been implicated in post-traumatic stress disorder, anxiety, and depression as well as chronic-stress related disorders and dysfunction in the human body. The frontal lobe comprises two-thirds of the human brain and function in language, memory, mood, affect, personality, moral reasoning, and attention.

The most exciting findings were extrapolated by Andrew Newberg, a radiologist who recruited study participants from various faith-based organizations, directing them to spend twelve minutes in active prayer—a conversation with God. His research demonstrated quantifiable changes in brain volume and metabolism, summarizing the

---

[33]

neurophysiological benefits of worship and prayer. Additional findings verify that incorporating prayer in the treatment plan for pathology ranging from hypertension to chronic inflammation has garnered robust results. The effect is accurately captured in 1 John 4:18 English Standard Version, "There is no fear in love but perfect love casts out fear."

The intrinsic personal and interpersonal nature of spirituality and religion are essential aspects of a multidimensional, holistic approach to positive aging that incorporates the mind, body, and spirit of the individual while factoring in their unique states of being. Consciously choosing the circumstance surrounding your everyday life promotes independence and dignity, which further accelerates successful aging.

There are so many things that improve with age. Wisdom and well-being goes up; stress levels and instability goes down. With specific aspects of memory, decision-making, empathy, self-confidence, body positivity, physical endurance, and female orgasm all on the upturn. Say "bye, bye" to negative emotions as feeling of loneliness, depression, anger, and boredom subside. Your ability to recall facts and figures most likely won't diminish as semantic memory is relativity resistant to the effect of aging.

If you're age sixty, chances are you're happier than you were in your forties. If that's true for you, own it; it's a good place to be. Researchers are debunking the once-common myths related to old age finding that happiness increases in the late fifties with the most blissful and euphoric times of life occurring in the sixties, seventies, and early eighties. Rest assured, there will be fewer sleep disturbances and less daytime fatigue. Plus you've finally gotten the parenting thing down so family ties have never mattered more.

You've gained comfort in who you are and clarity on your priorities with the most chaotic part of life behind you. Look at the final third of life with the same curiosity, creativity, and sense of positive possibility as you viewed the first two-thirds. Your best days may be ahead of you.

People are living decades longer due in part to medical innovations and advances in technology and public health, coupled with smarter health and lifestyle choices. According to a United Nations report, by 2050, the percentage of the US population age sixty-five and over is projected to increase by 20 percent. Therefore, our society in general and the health-care system in particular must advance its understanding of the needs of older adults and develop the resources with which to provide them. Our elders deserve to know how much we care.

Dr. Louise Aronson, author of *Elderhood: Redefining Aging, Transforming Medicine, Reimagining Life,* has a unique take on old age gleaned from her work as a geriatrician and professor of medicine at the University of California, San Francisco. Aronson insists that "we get more wrong (than right) when it comes to what it means to be . . . an aging, i.e., still-breathing human being."

"We've made old age into a disease, a condition to be dreaded, denigrated, neglected, and denied," said Aronson, who admits to experiencing vision loss, anxiety, arthritis, and other vestiges of aging. She challenges society and the medical field to see aging in a broader context.

The Hippocratic Oath, an oath of ethics historically taken by physicians states (in part), "I will abstain from all intentional wrongdoing and harm . . . I will keep pure and holy both my life and my art." It's a code of ethics, one might think, few patients benefit from especially the elderly.

"If we want old age to be something other than a loathsome expanse of years for decades," Aronson said, we need to examine the hows and whys of our current approach and develop a relevant plan of action that recognizes the full implications of our aging population.

Elders, you have to do your part. Prepare yourselves mentally, physically, and spiritually to live well (as best you can) from this moment forward. Designate time to finish all unfinished business whether in relationships or professional endeavors. Elderhood is a normal arc on the human developmental life span—a natural and fulfilling phase of life, as big and glorious and diverse as childhood and adolescence combined.

Deconstruct the "-isms" that inform your beliefs about getting old. Take back your power. Think about who you are and talk about who you are with enthusiasm and expectancy. Define another reality for yourself and other elders on the "come up." The Master is beckoning you to courageously enter territories that are as yet unexplored. Rejoice. Stand up, front and center as those around you. "Rise in the presence of the elderly," sayeth the Lord.

INTRODUCTION TO THE OVERTIME

No Holds Barred

The overtime is a free-form affair that rarely adapts to prescribed structure; only certain rules apply. *No holds barred* means "there are no limits; you're only effected by what you believe you can or cannot do. All stereotypes, be damned."

Make a commitment to truth-telling. Say what you want to say when you want to say it (thank you, king of comedy Bernie Mack). But before you say it, ask yourself, "Am I responding with kindness and care?" Be mindful; express only those things you are ready (and willing) to live.

You were raised up in the ways you should go, encouraged to use words with restraint, acknowledging that "life and death are in the power of the tongue, and those who love it will eat its fruit" (Proverbs 18:21 New American Standard Bible). There is no sense censoring yourself now. Tell it like it *really* is; activate truth's power to heal.

> *Elderliness is not a disease, but a richness.*
>
> —Kiganda proverb

You are neither bad-tempered, unproductive, and passive nor a babbling, depressed, and dementia-addled, old fogy versed in elderspeak or the alien or foreign species many young people make you out to be.

You are our moms, dads, nanas, revered and wise elders—self-defined, a union of elements (emotions, thoughts, and sensations) that constitute your individuality and identity. Your ancestors dot the globe.

You are a success, a captain of many industries. In a class by yourself with a brand of style—kid-skinned gloves, Jackie O. sunglasses, fedoras, ascots, Dapper Dan pocket squares, and a smile that's timeless.

No one ages identically, so the narrative must be privy to and capture your unique interior world where "-isms" born of gender, ethnicity, class, and denial are nullified by "been there, done that, God's still using me" sensibilities. Cancel entitlement, racism, biased assimilation, and attitude polarization. Resist the urge to evaluate new information through the prism/prison of preexisting beliefs.

When the contributions of those in middle and late adulthood and the oldest old are discounted, we are estranged from our humanity and a deeper connection to life and the ancestors. To arrive at this life span, you had to have made it through the earlier stages though maybe a little worse for the wear. Nevertheless, few have the level of authority that comes with advancing into elderhood with panache—spiritually, mentally, and physically whole. Like steak, old age can either be rare or well done.

Be in the moment. You're not out of time; you're part of a future defined by purpose, not peril. When you count yourself among the overtimers, remember you're still in the game. Tally up the points. It may be time to tie up loose ends, but there are still new threads to stitch and interlope even if it's to create an afghan that keeps you and the misses toasty and warm.

You only have one chance at this game called life, so invest your time wisely. Be fierce. Set up new rules. Slay them with finesse. Find ways to play harder; live happier and once will be enough.

TOUCH DOWN

It's the Overtime (Age 70+)

The elders of a community are the voice of God.

—Nigerian proverb

You've rowed your boat, taking turns as you gently sailed down the stream; jubilantly manifesting your dreams as life-giving waters move blessings to and through you. The secular has become sacred, and now you are empowered to call down God's mercy and grace like Moses did in Numbers 6:24–26.

The Lord bless you and keep you; the Lord make his
face shine on you and be gracious to you; the Lord
turn his face toward you and give you peace.

—Numbers 6:24–26 New International Version

You belong to God and are his instrument, utilizing the Father's earthly endowment to effortlessly evolve his purpose-driven plan. You are the source of self-regard that suffers no fools. The Yoruba call you *awọn alàgba*. The Zulu know you as *abadala*. "Come, *dattwa*," says the Hausa. The Swahili distinguish you as *mzee*. Your American sons and daughters of Africa honor you as our elder.

You've been through so much, answering to the names imposed upon us—colored, boy, nigger, coon, girl, the help, Negro, black, African American, and the list goes on. You have survived the physiological and psychological impact of racism and discrimination and the debilitating side effects caused by stress.

And still you rise—fully aligned with your human self, readily in the flow of divine order, trusting that each of your dimensions is a state of consciousness on your journey toward self-realization. Great revelations occur with everything that seeks transformation in your life rising to the surface.

For those seventy-plus, eighty, and oldest old highlighted in this life span, the urge to create (political change, secure civil/human rights, inspire activism, or share wisdom with the next generation etc.) is a juggernaut that is both demanding and invigorating. The aging brain of these elders is ideally suited to achieve such positive work. Diverse creative domains support the transition into fields that preserve wisdom and tap into the vast body of knowledge needed to construct culturally relevant and advanced works. Each of these individuals maintain awareness of a particular aspect of their environment, focusing on thoughts that inspire adaptive self-reflection. When one practices adaptive self-reflection, the focus is on the concrete parts of a situation and improvements that can be made. The ability to pay attention without distractions helped humans to survive and evolve since the beginning of time. Now, it's a skill that can assist those in the overtime to succeed in learning environments, at work, and in their relationships particularly where distraction-free environment exist.

Numerous studies suggest that highly creative individuals also employ a broadened, rather than focused, state of attention. This state of widened attention allows the individual to have disparate bits of information in mind simaltenaously. Combining that information may lessen the cumulative effect associated with experiencing everyday racism (every day, a phenomena that is said to change the brain function of both the oppressed and the oppressor, which sociologist Eric Jensen asserts is largely attributable to the interplay of chronic stress and neuroplasticity.

"The brain is constantly being shaped, wittingly and unwittingly, by environmental forces that impinge upon organisms. Among the influences on brain structure and function that are most powerful in inducing plastic change are social influences," the most consistent and ubiquitous being racism, according to researchers Richard Davidson (a professor of psychology at University of Wisconsin-Madison) and Bruce McEwen (neuroendocrinologist and head of the Harold and Margaret Milliken Hatch Laboratory of Neuroendocrinology at Rockefeller University).

Social justice scholar Philomena Essed dubbed "everyday racism" an extremely multifaceted yet surprisingly underacknowledged form of exclusion and oppression that is "integrated into routine practices of everyday life working through and in relation to gender, class, sexual orientation, and other domination systems." The intrinsic presumption of black inferiority, delusion of white superiority, and accompanying neuroplasticity somehow morphs into self-reinforced beliefs that are hardwired in the brain, leaving those who are not conscious (and aware) vulnerable to actions that confirm those false beliefs. Essed's later work theorized the concept of entitlement racism, which occurs when individuals feel they are allowed to say whatever they want, whenever they want, about whomever they want, in the name of freedom of expression. Entitlement racism links current politics to the "-isms" and other phobias that have historically plagued our nation: depictions of racism, white supremacy. Those in the overtime are painfully familiar with and well-equipped to challenge or change or ignore. Whether they are scaling mountain highs or ascending subterranean lows, the limitlessness of these melaninated icons is always in reemergence mode.

McArthur Binion

Many individuals in the overtime identified their passion and purpose early on, often maintaining long-term careers in anonymity, like seventy-two-year-old abstract painter McArthur Binion. Born in Mississippi and based in Illinois, Binion is an African American artist and former professor who has, over the course of his forty-year career, perfected his craft, attracting a level of acclaim for which the artist is more than worthy—an equitable trade off for the highly rewarding "do less, think more" approach many gifted artists employ.

Binion's work probes minimalism and personal identity, utilizing a core of grids, hand-drawn lines, and photocopied versions of his birth certificate in deeply original mathmetical art/equations personalized by blurring, complicating, and broadening the traditional idioms of abstraction, and modernism with autobiographical/ancestral memory. His work represents a confluence of influences, a web of black Southern heritage with the rhythmic cadence of black music, language, and literature threaded and swathed in West African fabric and textiles reminiscent of his mother's patchwork quilts.

The eleventh child of tenant farmer's nod to his Macon, Mississippi, roots and the rural modernist improvisational mash-up of his bebop abstractions, Binion eschews traditional brushes and paints, choosing a combination of oil sticks, Dixon wax crayons on aluminum, and laser-printed images instead to create ordered, textural, geometrically patterned compositions.

Binion's paintings serve as "guardians of a heritage that is both painful and poetic" and sons and daughters who shined like a thousand stars in the sky.

Maxine Moore Waters and Shirley Anita St. Hill Chisolm

Maxine Moore Waters is among the living legends who have walked the talk of overtime. This eighty years young "take no prisoner" US representative for California's Forty-Third Congressional District and member of the Democratic Party is now in her fifteenth term in the House. Her no-nonsense, no-holds-barred style of politics has garnered her the reputation of being the boldest (and bravest) legislator California has ever seen.

Unbought and unbossed like her predecessors, Waters realized the enormity of her potential and that she possessed an ability to size up her competition (and accomplishments) with discernment and objectivity. Naysayers predicted she would "crash and burn" having grown up poor and black, the fifth of thirteen children reared by a single mother in a St. Louis housing project.

An excerpt from her life story she recounted to students at her alma mater Vashon High School cautions them to "never fall victim to others predictions of failure; make liars out of them." Waters's high school yearbook included an early prediction that she would one day be speaker of the House of Representatives.

Waters began working at age thirteen in factories and segregated restaurants. Child labor could have easily deprived her of her childhood, realized potential, and dignity she so deserved. Working at such a young age did not interfere with her schooling or harm her physical and mental development.

Waters's honesty, rebellious nature, and immense ambition coupled with her willingness to confront life head on have served her well, posing her for a trajectory to that would propel her to heightened levels of success. She is self-confident, courageous, and commanding in whatever situation she finds herself in as others bask in her regal presence. Never reluctant to share her success, she is a powerful role model who sometimes finds others losing themselves and their identity in her mighty shadow.

In early adulthood, Waters placed emphasis on practical order and efficiency particularly in her professional life. She learned to cooperate with others, welcoming every opportunity to hear their opinions and the contributions they sought to make, noting the importance of listening very carefully to what people are trying to say (without commanding them) as a way to earn greater support and respect.

Midlife led Waters to an important crossroad, offering a turning point that highlighted her relationships, stimulating the creativity needed to activate her latent talents. Throughout her storied life, however, the key to Waters's success has been her ability to empathize with others and recognize that the right to personal autonomy is not anyone's sole preserve. As a result, she was able realize the ambitious and progressive vision that would birth within her the ability to lead and inspire others.

Waters stands on the shoulders of Shirley Anita St. Hill Chisholm— educator, author, and the first black woman elected to the United States Congress and the first woman and African American to seek the nomination for president of the United States (1972).

During her term of office, Fighting Shirley always took a stand advocating that "our children, our jobless men, our deprived, rejected, and starving fellow citizens must come first." For this reason, she said, I intend to vote no on every money bill that comes to the floor of this House that provides any funds to the Department of Defense." Chisholm was a woman of her word. She wanted history to remember her not for her monumental firsts but "as a black woman who lived in the twentieth century and dared to be herself."

Vernon Eulion Jordan Jr. and Benjamin Hooks

Vernon Eulion Jordan Jr. is an eighty-three-year-old attorney, business executive, civil rights activist, and influential figure in American politics. He was once considered one of the most prominent and outspoken black leaders in the country. After leaving private law practice in the early 1960s, Jordan became directly involved in activism in the field, serving as the Georgia field director for the NAACP, moving to the Southern Regional Council and later to the Voter Education Project.

In 1970, Jordan became executive director of the United Negro College Fund and served as president of the National Urban League (NUL) from 1971 to 1981. That year, he resigned from the NUL to take a position as legal counsel with a firm based in Washington, DC. Jordan faced the same uncertainty experienced by many black males in early adulthood who jumped at the chance to propel their hopes and dreams to the next level, oblivious to colorism and its "light, bright, damn near-white" requirements.

In African American oral history, the brown paper bag test served as a form of racial discrimination practiced within the black community that compared an individual's skin tone to the color of a brown paper bag, a test that was used to determine whether an individual could have access to certain admission and membership privileges. A test that is believed to be used by many African American social institutions such as sororities, fraternities, and churches. The term also references larger issues of class and social stratification within the black American culture, which Michael Eric Dyson examined in his book *Come Hell or High Water*.

"There is a curious color dynamic that persists in our culture. In fact, New Orleans invented the brown paper bag party—usually at a gathering in a home—where anyone darker than the bag attached to the door was denied entrance. The brown bag criterion survives as a metaphor for how the black cultural elite quite literally established caste along color lines within black life." A black color code Joy DeGruy says must be defeated by our love for one another.

At age forty-four, Jordan survived what could have easily precipitated a midlife crisis after being shot in the back by a rifleman who laid in wait as he emerged from his car. A critical shot that entered the middle of Jordan's back, between his chest cavities and his pelvis, which could have left him physically and psychologically disabled.

Racial disturbances similar to the succession of urban riots that followed the assassination of the Rev. Martin Luther King Jr. could have easily ensued. Had it not been for overtimers like President Jimmy Carter, Jesse Jackson, and others who had fought against the ravages of violence calming the sense of outrage and sadness that threatened to overtake the nation as black leaders like Jordan were being destroyed at every turn.

"We are here because we are hurt, we are traumatized, we are concerned," Jesse Jackson said. Jordan's wound, a seemingly well-placed shot by a professional, serve as a political statement much like the others.

Among those appealing for the black community to remain calm in the wake of the shooting was then executive director of the NAACP Benjamin Hooks, who, like Jordan, had far exceeded the low expectations America has for black boys and girls. He served as an attorney, preacher, Federal Communications Commission commissioner, criminal court judge, colleague, and lifelong friend to Jordan who spoke at his funeral in April 2010.

"The country has lost a great civil rights leader, and I've lost a very good friend," Jordan said. "He was open, honest, direct, straight, loved the Lord, loved the church. And he loved freedom."

Jordan's activism and business acumen continue to soar a body of work that began decades ago by Jordan, Hooks, and other black illuminaries.

Samella Lewis and Elizabeth Catlett

Art is not a luxury as many people think—it is a necessity. It documents history—it helps educate people and stores knowledge for generations to come.

—Dr. Samella Lewis

Samella Lewis came of age in a time when speaking up could result in dire consequences. Born in New Orleans, Louisiana, on February 27, 1923, Lewis refused to be complicit in her own marginalization, choosing Jim Crow as a moving target, a system Lewis would later be reprimanded for fighting to abolish. Time and time again, she made her voice heard despite negative reactions from others claiming that she had been "run out of places including Florida by its governor."

The print entitled "Field" shows a man standing under a massive etched (and circular) sun, his arms one slightly bent while the other jutting powerfully into the air, extended and clenched in a fist symbolic of the solidarity that existed between groups like the Black Panther Party and others in the Black Power movement. In this depiction, Lewis conjures up the plight of slaves and migrant workers.

Although an accomplished scholar, Lewis identifies herself first as an artist. During adolescence, Lewis spent time in the French Quarter, immersing herself in art and receiving private lessons free of charge. She would later enroll at Dillard University in 1940, where Elizabeth Catlett, then a young sculptor, served as her professor. Lewis was profoundly impacted by the lifelong sister/friendship she shared with Catlett, as it freed her imagination to run wild. Catlett wasn't demure as Southern-born Lewis was taught to be; she was bold with an affinity for her African ancestry and strong identity as a black woman artist and activist.

"Because I am a woman and know how a woman feels in body and mind, I sculpt, draw, and print women, generally black women. Many of my sculptures and prints deal with maternity because I am a mother and a grandmother," Catlett once said.

Born April 15, 1915, in Washington, DC, Catlett had, over the course of her seventy-year career, created work that sculpted our struggles for social justice, the revolutionary promise of black power, and the maternal instinct of black women as cultural gatekeepers into iconic images depicting the black experience in its full splendor. Catlett was able to obtain a scholarship from Hampton Institute for Lewis, who enthusiastically anticipated the support she might gain from attending an HBCU.

The image "Together We Stand" is enriched by Maya Angelou's poetic prose, a hand-embellished lithograph depicting six elders (three men, three women) dressed in woolen smocks, knobby trousers, overalls, and African patchwork dresses with shawls thrown over both shoulders and gelees, adorning their tresses with a male bent at the waist—his humongous hands holding the outstretched arms of a smiling little black girl.

"However I am perceived and deceived. However my ignorance and conceits, lay aside your fears that I will be undone, for I shall not be moved" is the meditation, signed and written in a circle on a grayish white canvas edged in kubo and raffia cloth.

Elizabeth Catlett died in 2012 at the age of ninety-six, prompting Lewis to share some heartfelt words of gratitude. "Elizabeth still lives in my life and my heart as my teacher and my friend. I will always remember her and be thankful for her friendship."

Lewis and Catlett's artistic collaboration lives on in the exhibition The Art of Elizabeth Catlett from the collection of Samella Lewis, a traveling exhibitions available for scheduling through 2020 featuring thirty works—sculptures and graphics by Catlett plus five works by her husband, artist Francisco Mora, and five works by Samella Lewis, which reunites Lewis and Catlett, two grand dames of African American art.

Just Going Forward

The years, the months, the days, and the hours have
flown by my open window. Here and here an incident, a

towering moment, a naked memory, an etched countenance,
a whisper in the dark, a golden glow these and much
more are the woven fabric of the time I have lived.

—Rev. Howard Washington Thurman

Dying and death are natural stages of human development—a metronome swinging back and forth, a meditative beat marking the rhythm of time. "For life and death are one," poet Kahlil Gibran once mused, "even as the river and the sea are one."

You may grapple with the realization that no one ever really dies. Finding consolation for this everlasting-to-everlasting journey is one we all have a stake in whether young or old, rich or poor.

There is much to do before you leave this place and answer death's clarion call. Life is calling you to access the inner depths of your being. Decode the words of author Zora Neale Hurston, "Grab your broom of anger and drive out the beast of fear." Make peace with the inevitability of your demise. Untangle the contents of your mind and discern life's deeper meaning. Unfold into the whole of who (and whose) you are—a dearly loved, inseparable, and essential aspect of the God of wonders.

Dive deep. Take those last great leaps to live out your purpose, even if only in your heart and soul. Acknowledge the triumphs, tribulations, and trepidations you've encountered. Calculate the sum total of your earthly endeavors.

Sing! Recite the lyrics to your soul's song. Rejoice! Hear God's voice serenading from within. Accomplish your legacy; do that one last thing you were born to do. Savor the precious, sweet moments that have yet to unfold. Psalm 90:3 (New King James Version) commands, "Return, O children of men." Your reawakening is near.

Dissecting the Fear

*I am listening to what fear teaches. I will never be gone.
I am a scar, a report from the front lines, a talisman, a
resurrection. A rough place on the chin of complacency.*

—Audre Lorde, poet,
essayist, feminist, and civil rights champion

Dying and death are subjects we are rarely encouraged to discuss. The words themselves are shrouded in euphemisms like *passing away* and *going home to meet one's maker*—that is, coded messages that we are programmed to use as we urgently strive to live, simultaneously observing the sand in the hourglass as it rapidly slips away.

Children think of death as a temporary state and do not comprehend that it is irreversible until they are between the ages of five and seven. Important concepts of reversibility, the universality of death, and the cessation of all functions develop at that time, according to developmental psychologist Jean Piaget.

Culture influences children's attitudes toward death with those living in impoverished environments, associating it with violence, while their middle-class counterparts connect it with disease, infirmity, and old age.

Caring adults can allay the anxiety a child might have by creating warm and safe environments to explore their individual feelings and experiences. It is important to keep in mind that children's cognitive readiness to understand dying and death varies.

Adolescents highly romanticize the concept of death. In their quest to discover and live out their identities, they maintain a sense of invincibility concerning themselves with how they will live, not how long which may explain the appeal of suicide during that life stage. However, when they must face their mortality because of terminal illness or critical injury, the emotional impact is far more intense as they contend with the certainty that their dreams will go unfulfilled.

It is in midlife that most people experience the full realization that they are indeed going to die. They may have already lost their parents and are now elders, the oldest generation in their families. This daunting shift in reality precipitates a profound change as they take stock of their careers, spousal relationships, parental successes and failures—contemplating their mortality and considering how to make the days, months, and years they have left really count. It is a powerful time to renew their commitment to life with vigor and zeal.

Generally those in late adulthood are far less anxiety-ridden about death, although it may appear as if the grim reaper is lurking at their door. The loss of friends and loved ones and the gradual diminishing of physical and mental health may signal a time to embrace and face death. But it can also be a wake-up call, a time to affirm the preciousness of life even as it is slipping away.

In African American culture, death is seen as part of the natural rhythm of life, which somewhat lessens the cultural fear around aging. Most enslaved Africans transported to the Americas could not carry on their traditions, although many of the rituals maintain similarity to those of their kinship group. For this reason, Karen H. Meyers writes in *The Truth about Death and Dying*, "African American funerals tend to be life-affirming and maintain a celebratory air intermingled with the sorrow."

Discovering a Purpose in Life and Death

You make known to me the path in life; in your presence there is fullness of joy; at your right hand are pleasures forevermore.

—Psalm 16:11 English Standard Version

It is the adults eighty-five and older, referred to as the oldest of the old, who have much to teach us about the circle of life. Most certainly, they have lost something—maybe their mobility, vision, hearing, memory, or even a spouse, children, and other loved ones—but they have not lost everything, particularly those things of significance like every day gratitude, joy, and happiness. Experiencing loss makes you far less anxious about life *and* death. To confront one's own demise is to come to terms with the magnificence of experiencing deeper and fuller lives from each moment to the next.

Many who are in the later stages of life refuse to be hidden away, segregated in "senior ghetto" nursing homes or retirement communities, choosing instead to maintain their independence and a willfulness to live life on their own terms. Eighty-five can be the new sixty if you stay physically active, socially engaged, consume a plant-based diet, and train your brain.

Untapped Melodies

> *Lord, make me to know my end and what*
> *is the measure of my days.*
>
> —Psalm 39:4 (New King James Version)

Hidden memories can resurface when those who are facing death intentionally create life reviews, remembrances that honor the significant people, incidents, and experiences that have created spaces of joy and contentment. This profoundly therapeutic process, somewhat like a bucket list, can be expressed through written and taped autobiographies, and it pilgrimages back to locations where important stages of their lives were played out—reunions, scrapbooking, or genealogy research on their ethnic origins. "There is no need to be afraid of death," psychiatrist Elisabeth Kübler-Ross once wrote. "Cognizance of death," she said, "is the key that unlocks the door to personal growth and unleashes the development of human potentiality."

Dare to live intentionally while dying. It is a courageous act of faith. Be compassionate and empathetic. Own the procession of emotions that may emerge like those captured in *A Burst of Light: and Other Essays* by Audre Lorde.

> We all have to die at least once. Making that death useful would be winning for me. I wasn't supposed to exist anyway, not in any meaningful way in this . . . world. I want desperately to live, and I'm ready to fight for that living even if I die shortly. Just writing those words down snaps everything I want to do into a neon clarity . . . For the first time, I really feel that my writing has a substance and stature that will survive me.

> I want to live the rest of my life, however long or short, with as much sweetness as I can decently manage, loving all the people I love, and doing as much as I can of the work I still have to do. I am going to write fire until it comes out my ears, my eyes, my nose holes—everywhere. Until it's every breath I breathe. I'm going to go out like a meteor!

The influence of culture on health can be utilized as a rehabilitative tool. Culture positively affects perceptions of health, illness and death, beliefs about disease causation, and appropriate approaches to health promotion and how illness and pain are experienced and expressed. Cultural competencies promote trust and improve health care and treatment adherence.

The collectivistic characteristics of the African diaspora culture focuses on *we*, promotes relatedness and interdependence, connects the family, values respect and obedience, and emphasizes group goals, cooperation, and harmony—noting the greater, broader influence of group views and values.

Floyd L. Griffin Jr.

Bereavement and Grief—Just Going Forward

Be a mountain or lean on one.

—Somali proverb

Death is difficult not only for the dying but for those left behind. The experiences and expressions of grief and their physical, emotional, psychological, and spiritual implications vary between individuals and across culture.

"Out with the old, in with the new" is out of alignment with the cultural consciousness of African Americans who acknowledge the authority of the elders and pay homage to their wisdom. Favor is rarely bestowed upon the frivolous, all-about-me alternative.

Research reveals that African Americans have a greater acceptance of death, seeing it as a part of a continuum of life, a transition between one world and the next. Blacks go through more bereavement by homicide and accidents, experience significant negative impact on their self-identity, grieve more for the loss of extended kin, maintain an ongoing spiritual connection with the deceased, and intuit a sense of support in that grief, not expressing complex symptoms with others or seeking professional support but instead relying on their multigenerational village to guide them through the crisis. Religion provides a means for comprehending and accepting loss, facilitating a transformed and enduring connection to the deceased. More than any other ethnic group, African Americans are a deeply religious, God-fearing people. Our unshakable belief sustains our continual faith as captured in the "community, other mother," words of poet Lucille Clifton.

Our community has historically demonstrated remarkable resilience by turning within and utilizing ancestral grieving practices that reflect our never-ceasing faith in the power, protection, and privilege associated with being the sons and daughters of the Most High God.

Our spiritual beliefs and psychological well-being are intrinsically linked. Despite all efforts to diminish us at every turn, we remain brave and unbossed, and *still we rise*!

The melding of this tried-and-true spirit-mind-body praxis may offer the relief we need as we seek to understand, proactively respond to, and administer the corrective measures that will ensure that our needs and those of our families, loved ones, and communities are met.

Dying with Dignity

> *Everyone you love, everyone you know, everyone you ever heard of, every human being who ever was, lived out their lives on this mote of dirt suspended in a sunbeam.*
>
> —Carl Edward Sagan,
> astronomer, cosmologist, astrophysicist, and author

Most African American families believe that when loved ones are facing the end of their lives, it is their responsibility to be the primary caregiver—a choice that reflects African traditions and the covenant we've made to God and one another. When we attend to those who are dying, we realize how much love matters. Our presence shows our loved ones that they count and that they are viable, living human beings up until their last breath and have added immeasurably to life's repository of wisdom and grace. We can help them embrace their circumstances by acknowledging the reality of their dying, allowing them to take the lead in those difficult discussions and expressing our emotions, which frees them to be honest about their own feelings.

When lovingly dispensed, even music can become a prescriptive instrument that ministers to the body, emotions, and spirit of those who are dying and their loved ones. Music replicates the body's capacity to sing, vibrate, and activate rhythms in the universe. To hear music is like a homecoming, allowing us to resonate with who we are as human beings. Knowing that our presence means more than mere words can convey is powerful and liberating. Expressions of gratitude, forgiveness, and recollection of love that has been their sustenance emerge. Listen intensely for any messages they may want to share, and you may find answers to your own life questions.

However, our loved ones may be struggling with physical and mental challenges that we are ill-equipped to handle, which may result in their placement in a senior facility, where proper care can be administered. Feelings of guilt or fear that they will be at risk may surface. If so, share your concerns with health professionals, confide in the people in your village, and seek guidance from a religious leader you trust. Keep loving them, even if at a distance. It's a gift that both of you can share.

There is a psychology to death according to psychiatrist Elisabeth Kübler-Ross, whose pioneering work stimulated interest in the stages of death and dying. She found out that most of her patients welcomed the opportunity to speak authentically about their condition, maintaining a keen awareness of their proximity to death even when that diagnosis had never been shared.

Based on these discussions, Kübler-Ross theorized that there are five stages in coming to terms with our impermanence during this final phase of growth: (1) denial—refusal to accept the reality of what is occurring, that when allowed some hope and given the assurance that they will not be abandoned, the initial shock and denial quickly dissipates; (2) anger—the essential need to express the rage; (3) bargaining for extra time, an acknowledgment that time is limited and life is finite; (4) depression often offset by expressing the depths of their anguish; and (5) ultimate acceptance and a feeling of peace with themselves and the world. The sequence in which these stages occur may vary.

This sense of acceptance and finality Kübler-Ross refers to is reflected in the life and death of John Mose Willis, who died while on his knees in prayer. Just shy of "oldest of old" status, this Mississippi–born and bred father of three and grandfather of two overcame his own father's death before his birth and the demise of his mother at age thirteen. Rising above his circumstance through sheer will and a "come hell or high water" determination. Such is our glorious inheritance.

From the Soul

The life of the dead is placed in the memory of the living.

—Marcus Tullius Cicero, Roman statesman

Our hard-earned skepticism and righteous indignation come as a result of a history of medical abuse, unequal treatment, and racially motivated medical experimentation we've unknowingly been participants in.

This centuries-old opposition is rooted in the involuntary sterilizations of black women, the Tuskegee syphilis experiment, and Henrietta Lacks, whose cancer cells (stolen without her permission in 1951) are the source of the HeLa cell line, the first immortalized and most important cell line in medical research. Her cells have spawned over seventeen thousand patents that have contributed to "research on the effects of zero gravity in outer space, the development of the polio vaccine and used in scientific landmarks such as cloning, gene mapping, and *in vitro* fertilization," contributing to medical breakthroughs that benefited the researchers at the exclusion of the black subjects. It is just a sampling of the medical apartheid black people have endured.

It's important that we claim all the ugly details.
So we can create something beautiful.

—Bryan Stevenson, lawyer, social justice activist,
founder and executive director of the Equal Justice Initiative

Because of the challenges we've faced, we are reluctant to place the health of our loved ones in the hands of physicians or consider contemporary end-of-life systems, such as hospice and palliative care, as viable options. Palliative care is a therapeutic approach that is said to improve the quality of life of patients facing life-threatening illness and their physical, psychosocial, and spiritual effects.

Although hospice is associated with better communication, symptom management, caregiver support, and overall satisfaction for terminally ill patients and their families, Dr. Kimberly Johnson, associate professor of medicine (geriatrics) at Duke University School of Medicine, says there are "a number of factors that may explain the lower rate of utilization by African Americans" including patient knowledge about hospice care, treatment preferences, cultural and spiritual beliefs, and the need to restore trust in the health-care system.

Instead, many African American continue to advocate for aggressive life-sustaining interventions, such as resuscitation and mechanical ventilation (up until the very end) even when there's little chance of survival. The responsibility to better explain the motivation behind those crucial end-of-life decisions must not rest with the physicians who treat them—particularly when their biases may contribute to the health disparities.

Partnerships with faith-based organizations, engagement of African American volunteers and staff, education, and outreach and alliances with health advocates may be the key to offset this trend.

For those who seek to support their loved ones in this transition, Five Wishes, a global initiative of Aging with Dignity, lets families and physicians know the following:

1. Who you want to make health-care decisions for you when you can't make them for yourself
2. The kind of medical treatment you want or don't want

3. How comfortable you want to be
4. How you want people to treat you
5. What you want your loved ones to know

Our Cultural Perspectives

Ancestorhood is ritualized throughout the stages of life in rites of passage that govern initiation, marriage, birth, and death. Once we transition, our ancient cultures provide a template for the next realm of existence. Sacred texts such as the Tibetan Book of the Dead are read to the dearly departed over a period of forty-nine days to instruct them on how to travel through the afterlife to attain freedom.

Our own creation narratives can be seen in the book of Genesis where God is described as the creator and Adam is advised "you shall surely die," (Genesis 2:17 New King James Version) at the moment of his disobedience when he ate from the forbidden tree.

Broadening our cultural landscape allows us to include the creation stories of the Maori, whose goddess Hinetitama, the goddess of the dawn, is the same deity who embodies Hine-nui-te-pō, the goddess of the darkness, who guides souls across the threshold of death.

An angel of destiny or guardian spirit that arrived at the time of conception is said to reappear at the end of our earthly life to remind us of our divine nature and that someone who loves us dearly will be there to help us enter the next stage of existence. Our spiritual guides assist the souls in avoiding delays and interruptions in this mystical afterlife journey.

Many of the contemporary customs and traditions we practice, as it relates to death and burials, can be traced back to the Bakongo people of southern Congo, who accept life and death as a continuum of existence, with death viewed as another state of being where the deceased inhabits the spirit world. These rituals (guided by the

African beliefs associated with after-death existence and the power and purpose of the deceased) are deeply rooted in the culture, customs, and indigenous religions of the continent. Traditions in the form of verbal expression, superstitions, religious practices, and auditory communication have survived among people of African descent in the Caribbean and the Americas. After death has been confirmed, every relative and friend of the deceased is contacted. They moan, holler, wail, faint, fall out, and begin the lengthy undertaking of processing death after life. All mirrors, windows, and reflective surfaces in the home must be covered and all pictures turned to face the wall. Every effort is made to conduct their going-home ceremony on a sunny day.

Typically, there is a five-to-seven-day mourning period then a wake that may take place at the funeral parlor, church, or home of the deceased prior to the funeral, which may include a procession. All the cars in the procession place purple flags upon their antennas and drive with the headlights on to identify themselves as members of the assemblage. The immediate family remains silent during the burial and stands on one side of the grave site, with the community on the other.

There are ceremonial traditions concerning the actual burial that include making sure the deceased's feet face the east to allow their rising at Judgment Day. Coins can be placed either on the eyes or in their hands representing their contributions to the community of the ancestors or as a token for admittance to the spirit world, with additional coins placed on or around the grave site.

The specific ways we respond to death and the importance placed on the deceased being properly put to rest ensures his spirit will be at peace and his place in the community of ancestors will be secured, a supremely valued tradition in the African belief system. These cultural precepts will continue to feed our souls and be transformed into an embedded beat that reverberates in our collective hearts. The memory of our divine natural arrangement (DNA) has profound potency.

I have done good work. There is a hell of a lot more I have to do . . . I feel I still have enough moxie to do it all, on whatever terms I'm dealt, timely or not. Enough moxie to chew the whole world up and spit it out in bite-sized pieces, useful and warm and wet and delectable because they came out of my mouth.

—Audre Lorde

We Are Who We've Been Waiting For

Our greatest power lies dormant within us. We must tap into that cosmic, supernatural acuity to live and prosper against obstacles that have vanquished others of a lesser hue. This is our Sankofa moment—a divined time to reach back and fetch our ancient wisdom and the culture that has been the key to our collective healing since the dawn of this time/space reality. In the eloquent words of Maya Angelou, "We must confess that we are the possible, we are the miraculous, the true wonder of this world!"

Funeral Prearrangement Planning

There's an old saying that goes, "Nothing is certain in life except death and taxes." The Internal Revenue Service is happy to help with your taxes, but what about your death? That's where your licensed and professional funeral directors can help. When death occurs, everyone has certain obligations, although there are only three things that must be done:

- The deceased must be removed from the place of death.
- A death certificate must be completed and properly filed with the Bureau of Vital Statistics.
- A member of the immediate family/survivors must decide what is to be done with the deceased.

Whether it involves a funeral service, cremation service, or memorial service. Funerals are for the living. They offer social support by providing a time and place for family and friends to come together in a way to show solace and support. Visitation of the deceased by both family and friends creates a time and place for sharing the experiences of a life well lived. Both the visitation and viewing help survivors begin to fully accept the reality that death has occurred.

Many people feel that their family, other survivors, or friends already know what to do and will be able to adequately handle things when the time arrives. Unfortunately, this is not often the case. Worry can lead survivors into needless frustration, anxiety, nervousness, deeper pain, and grief when faced with having to make funeral arrangements immediately upon their loved one's death. When the stark reality of death unexpectedly invades our lives, we need time to adjust. If funeral and final disposition arrangements must be immediately considered, under pressure or time constraints, many wishes of the deceased and the survivors may be overlooked.

Why put your loved ones through this when there's a better way? Perhaps, one of the noblest acts a person can do for their family is to make funeral prearrangements.

Making funeral prearrangements is the simple and secure way to provide for the eventual tomorrow. It just makes good sense. Funeral prearrangement is the careful, thoughtful planning of funeral services before the need arises.

Making funeral prearrangements provides necessary information for the death certificate as well as for the funeral director, cemeterian, and all others who will need essential information quickly. It provides the opportunity for you and your family to fully consider the events and requirements accompanying a death beforehand.

It allows you to determine the exact type and extent of funeral, cremation, or memorial arrangements you desire. There are many possibilities for you to consider as you decide what is to be done.

Every decision made should include consideration for the survivors, your religious beliefs, your finances, and the legal requirements of the state. Your funeral director can be a source of guidance in these matters, but the choices are solely yours.

Word to the wise: only a state-licensed, professional funeral director can lawfully and rightfully assist you with such vital matters. To ensure an individual's validity, ask to see their credentials and/or call your local funeral director.

Another added value of making funeral prearrangements is that it determines the costs involved for burial, cremation, memorial, or other arrangements based on your personal desires. All costs can be kept in line with your budget.

There is another key factor to consider regarding funeral prearrangements—the unfortunate fact that some of us may outlive our financial assets. When this happens, even the most affluent among us can find themselves in such a position.

As readily available funds for living dwindle away to nothing, it becomes even more apparent that funding even the most austere funeral ceremony would be difficult, if not impossible. There is no one who truly wants a pauper's (public aid–funded) funeral.

Fortunately, the government has provided a way for dignity to be preserved so that individuals or a family facing this situation may avoid a public-aid funeral. Planning is the key. Properly arranged and funded, dignity and peace of mind can be maintained through the end of life and beyond for the survivors.

Making a funeral prearrangement plan is simple. You merely sit down with your licensed local professional funeral director and carefully review your entire funeral and cremation service options. Discuss your wishes and desires, and select the manner in which you will pay for the arrangements made. You will receive detailed written documents to retain for your permanent records and those of your family.

There is no cost involved in making a funeral prearrangement plan. The consultation session and subsequent written documents are free of charge.

Funeral prearrangement does not require prepayment. However, once you have decided exactly what you want, you may wish to wisely take advantage of the benefits of prepayment in order to spare your survivors any financial hardship or worries. Prepayment also helps guard against inflation, allowing you to use existing life insurance benefits for ongoing family support and future living expenses. Your money is protected and safeguarded. Most state attorney general offices and various other state and federal agencies carefully oversee all funds set aside for future final expenses.

What if I change my mind about who I want to perform my services or I move out of the area? No problem. Your funds, in most cases, are completely transferable to any acceptable provider of your choice anywhere in the continental United States.

Who should consider funeral preplanning? It should be considered by people who feel a need or desire to plan ahead.

These may include

- individuals who have no close living relatives,
- individuals who have no survivors,
- people who move away from home but wish to have final rites in their former community,
- families who feel planning their funeral and burial arrangement would be a valuable shared experience,
- parents who wish to give their children guidance in making funeral arrangements,

- those who travel considerably, and
- anyone with a sincere desire to make things easier for their loved ones and give them real peace of mind.

> *Keep in mind there is no "right" way to arrange*
> *a funeral service. Different people have differing*
> *opinions. You will know what is right for you.*

—Christopher Kuhnen, licensed funeral director

Time to Give Careful Consideration to End-of-Life Planning

Most of us are guilty of procrastinating when it comes to getting all our final affairs in order. Here are some things you need to consider today to ensure your affairs are in proper order when the worst happens:

1. Consider getting an attorney, not just any attorney but a specialist. An attorney skilled in handling estates can be an invaluable asset. For married couples, it may be a good idea for each spouse to get their own attorney. Even in a good marriage, there may be issues that each party wishes to discuss in private, such as how to protect the children in the event of a remarriage.

2. Collect all original documents and review them yearly.

3. Do you know where all your insurance policies are? Have you checked your life insurance policies? Are your beneficiary designations current on those policies? If not, make sure to change them to who you desire. When was the last time you checked? It is a good idea to review these documents every few years. Make sure that your original choices reflect your current realities.

4. Where is the deed to your house? Car title? Other important papers? Locate and collect them all, and make sure they are all current and express your desires. If you take the time to keep them in order, it will save you both time and money later and help you make sure that nothing is overlooked or missing.

Do You Have a Will?

Why do we need a will? People use them to write down family members whom they want to provide for when they die and how they want to distribute what they own. Wills also let us specify someone we would like to look after our kids or to leave personal gifts and meaningful things to people or organizations we choose. Discuss whether you need a trust for your minor children. If you don't have a will, this could put our families into legal and financial difficulties.

Don't Have a Will or Need to Update a Previous Will?

You can get one drafted by someone with experience, such as a lawyer or trustee company. A will must also be signed and witnessed. If the proper procedures are not followed, a will may not be valid. Wills don't have to be pricey. Some lawyers will even write one for free, so there's no harm asking around. There are also many free generic will templates online you can download and complete.

Where Is Your Durable Health-Care Power of Attorney?

The durable health-care power of attorney is the health-care document that allows you to designate someone who will make health-care decisions for you if you are unable to do so. Have you discussed this with the person you chose? The best time to discuss this is when you are healthy and rational. Whether you are discussing this with your children, wife, husband, your partner, or your parents, take the time to express what you really want so they will not have to guess should the need arose. Send a notarized copy of your wishes to your family physician and attorney, and make sure everyone knows where this document is kept.

Disability Insurance

Do you have it? If you are working, you have an income to protect. Sometimes we forget that the worst-case scenario is not if we die but if we are critically disabled and unable to work. A two-income family needs adequate protection on both incomes—this should be priority. Disability insurance is only available when you can substantiate your income and when you are healthy and don't need it. Educate yourself on how to protect your earning power.

Write a Letter to Your Designated Guardian

If you have minor children, you will include a designation in your will for both a guardian and an alternate guardian. Usually, this is the other parent. But given the importance of this responsibility, you must take the time to discuss this at length with the designee and select at least one alternate. Write a long letter that delineates your personal feelings on key issues from Sunday school and religion to educational priorities for your children. It may be difficult to do now. But should the need arise, the letter will serve as a crucial resource in very trying times.

Protect Your Children

What happens if you leave everything to your spouse—you die first— and they remarry? How are your children protected? Things happen, and people change. Sentimental items should be given specifically to the person of your choice. Because if you simply leave everything to your spouse, you have no way to ensure that those items will, years later, go where you want. Don't leave it to chance.

Consider Your Parents in Your Long-Term Planning

Will they require long-term care? Are you going to have to help them if they do need long-term care? Have funeral prearrangements been made for them? Who will make these decisions when the time comes? Taking care of elderly parents when college tuition also comes due can create a heavy burden on any family. Help your parents sort out these issues now, or you may be responsible by default and in serious difficulty later.

Consider What Total Insurance Coverage You Could Use

Insurance offers you protection for pennies on the dollar. For the cost of a good shopping spree every year, you can create an immediate estate that can protect your children, even if you never save another penny. Consider a small policy that can protect your mortgage if something happens to your partner. When you have your family discussion, make sure you understand what insurance is in place and consider what areas are not protected.

Talk to Your Spouse or Partner

Talking to your spouse or partner about these issues is the last thing on anyone's list. But we need to make sure that everything is in order and that we do not operate under blind assumptions that can hurt us later because they are incorrect. After you have organized the papers you can find, set a time to review your plans and make a list of questions that need to be answered. Explain the fears you have about any topic and consider the choices that you can make together. It is unfair to assume that your spouse or partner will take care of this alone. Don't assume—ask and discuss all issues openly.

—Christopher Kuhnen,
licensed funeral director, contributor

THE EPILOGUE

My Quarter Memoir—Life: Four Quarters plus Overtime

"What the generation to come might know them,
even the children which should be born; who should
arise and declare to them their children".

(Psalms 78:6 King James Version)

Introduction

Life: Four Quarters plus Overtime memoir represents the making of the man that I am in the overtime of my life. These memoirs are personal reflections and snapshots of my life's journey, quarter by quarter, to the overtime. I begin in quarter 1 by sharing memories from my life as a child in Milledgeville, Georgia, which began with my parents instilling in me and my brother and sister (at a young age) what it would take to truly succeed in life. I then reflect on quarters 2, 3, and 4, where I share snapshots from my young adult life as a student at Tuskegee University and the beginning of my journey to becoming a husband to the love of my life, Nathalie, and as a father and grandfather; my rise through the ranks of becoming a military officer; and my time as an entrepreneur in my family business and in politics. These reflections culminate in the overtime of life with my personal recommendations on living a fulfilling life during these years, the golden years! This is my gift to the nation. Given with heartfelt love and concern, I hope it serves as a game-changing resource of positive, purposeful information for this generation and those yet unborn, as they design the vision for their life: four quarters plus overtime. While these memoirs offer a glimpse into each quarter and the overtime of my life, the autobiography *Legacy to Legend: Winners Make It Happen*, which I penned in 2008, will give you an in-depth look at my life from the first quarter to the later years of the fourth quarter.

First Quarter (Birth to Seventeen)—Growing Up Under Good Guidance

There's no doubt that the village in Milledgeville, Georgia, was real and pretty much like most cities and towns during segregation, where most black people lived among other black people. It was a time in which family members lived close by and neighbors acted like family members. They made sure that young people carried themselves respectfully. When you did something wrong away from home, you were scolded, and when you made it home, you got it again. The village concept is relevant. It should be in effect and working today, but you don't have the closeness and connection that we had when I was coming up. A lot of this has to do with where we live. Diversity is good, but we don't really know one another like we did when I was coming up. It's one of the downsides of not having a village concept happening today. If the village was real today, we would have folks in different age groups mentoring and supporting young people to help change the community at large. For example, our teachers were a tremendous resource. They were dedicated to ensuring that we got the best education available within the environment we were growing up and were considered upstanding people that could be counted on. In addition, you had leaders from organizations like the National Association for the Advancement of Colored People (NAACP), the Southern Christian Leadership Conference (SCLC), the union, and fraternities and sororities that wanted us to do well while in school as we entered the second quarter of life. You never forget the impact these people have on your life. For me, it was Ella Beaner Lee. Ella taught Sunday school at our church (Union Baptist), and under her, we presided over church activities like the Easter program and vacation Bible school. This helped to develop our leadership skills.

It still takes a village, but because of societal change and the breakdown of the traditional family, it cannot be the same village. Parents are no longer involved in getting children engaged in activities in the church and are, in fact, absent. Black men are almost invisible. The family nucleus is not what it was during the first quarter of my life. Positive things are happening in our communities, but children must be involved. Each one teach one! There are a lot of positive things children can be a part of—there must be more than just sports and playing video games. Exposing adolescents to various positive extracurricular activities and hobbies can help detour them from becoming involved in negative activities young people sometimes become involved in (drugs, alcohol, gangs, skipping school). There are many encouraging and inspiring activities your child can participate in depending on their interest and age.

The Power of Integrity, Honesty, Responsibility, and Loyalty Through Service

Serving others fosters integrity, honesty, responsibility, and loyalty— service is powerful! For children to be successful in life, parents must start early in a variety of ways. It wasn't something my parents taught us from a book; it was lived by them every day. Both our parents were entrepreneurs, and we watched how they dealt with people and how they carried themselves. We, too, were expected to model these same behaviors, and if we didn't, they would let us know immediately. How you carry yourself is of the upmost importance. It's your signature and part of your legacy. For instance, you can't go out and get a job if employers don't trust you or feel that you're not being honest or that you have no integrity, especially if you have a desire to move up the ladder in your chosen field. So it's extremely important to have those things in place. How much integrity, honesty, responsibility, and loyalty you possess determines whether you will serve others.

Overcoming Childhood Obstacles

I didn't have a lot of distractions coming up through middle and high school. We had friends and classmates, and our closeness help cut back on conflicts. Kids today have a whole different level of distractions. I didn't know that much about drugs until I went into the military. If young people were selling or doing drugs, it was kept under wraps. We didn't have cars to run the streets, and our parents always knew where we were and what we were doing. Therefore, I didn't have any major problems related to the challenges today's youth face. One solution is to find a mentor. Mentors serve as an additional adult who can be trusted to guide and lead a young person, someone who can be depended on and can offer trusted advice. Children and teenagers must see that there are a number of adults who care for them and their futures and who will step up to the plate during times of struggle. The mentor chosen should be older and more experienced, someone who has "been there, done that," and someone you can lean on to help you through difficult times. Adults shouldn't get to the third quarter of life wishing they'd had someone to tell them that the road they were on was going nowhere.

Influence Through Observation

I don't remember the exact age that I was impacted by what I observed, but around age eight, my parents built a concrete block grocery store next to the house. They hired black contractors who included masons, carpenters, plumbers, electricians, and finishers. I was so thrilled to see them coming out and constructing the building. This was the catalyst that sparked my interest in pursuing a career in construction. As a young child growing up in a tight-knit community, I also knew when anyone had come home to visit after moving away. While this was always interesting, I was especially intrigued with the young men who would come home from the army. On Sunday morning, they would wear their freshly pressed uniforms and shoes that were so shiny you could see your face in them. I thought to myself, *One day I'm going to look mighty spiffy in one of those uniforms.* This was during the Korean War, and it made such an impression on me that I remember these times vividly. After watching these soldiers, I said to my parents, "I want to go into the military too!" During high school, I decided that I wanted to go to college as well. To accomplish both goals of construction and military careers, I chose Tuskegee Institute; I could be commissioned as an officer in their ROTC program while pursuing a building construction–related concentration of courses. So, you see, it was in the early years of the first quarter of life that I decided what I wanted to become when I grew up.

The Advantage of Deciding and Pursuing Your Professional Path Early

Once again, it goes back to parents. They didn't really have to motivate me; I simply observed them running their business. When I shared my life plans with them, they supported me wholeheartedly. Both my parents were very clear role models in integrity combined with hard work and perseverance, so I received this modeling early on. Unfortunately, many young people today do not have this luxury, and someone in the village needs to step up to the plate and help to equip our future leaders during the first quarter of their lives with the tools that will carry them successfully through the remaining quarters until they reach overtime.

Mentors and role models can build a good foundation in a young person in a variety of ways. Most communities offer an array of interesting things to explore—tap into the arts and culture environment, visit the library and museums, attend live theater. College tours and job fairs can open a young adult's eyes to a myriad of possibilities, stoking the imagination and creating passion and desire. Parents and mentors can build confidence in a young that he/she can be or do anything, if they can only dream it. High school doesn't last forever, and knowing your child's interests and skills can go a long way toward offering appropriate and interesting avenues to explore. In this way, young people have at least a general idea of the direction they would like to take when they reach the second quarter of life.

The World Is Bigger Than Where You Are

Children should be living like the world is bigger than where they live. I had a general idea that the world was bigger than Milledgeville because of our family vacations to Florida to visit my paternal aunt who owned businesses there. I also gained exposure to the world from my relatives who lived up north, in places like New York and Cleveland. Although I didn't visit those areas, they would come home to Milledgeville during the summer, and my cousins and I would have conversations about our respective hometowns. We didn't have a lot to draw from on television like today's youth, but I would watch Channel 13 (WMAZ) in Macon, Georgia; it was the only channel we could get.

After being gone from Milledgeville for twenty-eight years, I returned and began working with the 100 Black Men of America. Once, when we were taking a group of boys to an Atlanta Braves game, we passed through Eatonton, Georgia, about ten miles from Milledgeville. I overheard some of the boys saying, "Look at these buildings! Are we in Atlanta yet?" It was very telling—these kids had not been anywhere away from their home villages. There are kids who have never been out of Milledgeville. Traveling away from one's hometown, whether it be a ball game or a museum in Atlanta, opens children's eyes to the size of the world and helps them imagine what life could be like for them.

Solve Your Problems Peacefully
We didn't have much conflict growing, mostly a little bit of cursing here and there. We were equipped with the conflict-resolution tools needed to solve our disagreements peacefully and move on. When we were young, there was a healthy respect for what our parents wanted us to do, and getting into trouble was not an option. So if we had beef with someone, it didn't escalate or last long. In today's society, it's much more difficult for the youth to peacefully resolve their differences. Senseless deaths among our youth have become all too common with the ease in which teens are able to get their hands on a firearm. We have too many children (and grandchildren) raising children and too many parents who want to be their children's friend. Parents give and give to their children without requiring them

to earn what they receive. This has resulted in a generation of youth who don't understand the value of a dollar and don't appreciate what they have. When you combine the mind-set of "I can have whatever I want" with the ease of acquiring a handgun and no tools for conflict resolution, the end result is often the death of a teen at the hands of another teen.

Breaking the Chain of Poverty
We also have too many families trying to keep up with the Joneses. Some of this happened when I was growing up. If you don't have a BMW or Mercedes and you are living in a mobile home, then you feel that you're a nobody and that you don't measure up to those who do. We must change this mind-set, or it will perpetuate for generations to come.

As a people who constantly consume and never save money, we aren't leaving a significant legacy for future generations. Generational wealth doesn't necessarily mean having a million dollars in the bank to leave your children; it simply means that you do have *something*. Teaching children that there is value in building an economic future for yourself (and for them when you are gone) teaches the value of acquiring and saving. When I was growing up, we had some black businesses that included grocery stores, construction companies, and other businesses. It's very difficult to find skilled black specialists now. Why is this? We need more young blacks who aspire to have an education and venture into entrepreneurship; we are industrious and highly capable, and our youth should be capitalizing on our innate abilities and strength. We must prioritize and recommit to economic greatness again.

Education—The More You Know, The More You Grow
The power of education kicked in early in my life. When I was growing up, a lot of schooling was being done through the churches. I attended a small church on the same block that I lived; I even started earlier than I should have. I will never forget Mrs. Ray; she taught several grade levels in this one small building. However, this was not

the only education I received; my parents took me places outside of Milledgeville to open up my mind. Children who stay inside all day and play video games will not advance; children must be exposed to a variety of experiences so their minds can wander. Middle Georgia is full of opportunities for children to learn about the world. In Macon alone, there is the Georgia Sports Hall of Fame (for those who like sports), the Tubman Museum for children to learn about our history, and the Museum of Arts and Sciences, where children can learn about arts and culture and about the skies. There is also the Museum of Aviation in Warner Robins, where most boys and girls love to learn about airplanes. There are all kinds of places you can take children today. Today's children have a much greater chance to advance their education than when I was growing up.

Words of Wisdom Work

Growing up in Milledgeville had a great impact on me because of the elderly people who encouraged us to go out into the world and do great things. Even though we were living in a segregated society, we were expected to do great things. There were a lot of people out there who felt things would change. My grandfather on my father's side was one hundred years old when he died. He was also a minister. I never will forget him telling us, "You all need to get as much education as possible. One day it won't be this way. When things get better, you need to be ready." Although he couldn't read well, he could discern the Bible and was a businessman (he delivered coal all over the community). These words of wisdom from him and others shaped our thinking and let us know that we could succeed even with all the challenges we faced. Young people today need similar resources. Adults must be willing to engage them and provide something of substance that will make a difference in their lives and serve as a resource when they need guidance.

Up, Up and Away

Academically, my focus during my last year of high school was taking classes that would prepare me for college. I placed an emphasis on mathematics, especially geometry and trigonometry because those subjects would be needed in college. Socially, I attended the prom and most of the cotillion balls in Macon, Georgia, sponsored by the Alpha Phi Alpha fraternity. To receive an invitation to escort the young ladies participating in the cotillion balls, young men had to be ethical and upstanding. I also participated in football, band, and the choir. However, it was academics and the desire to attend Tuskegee Institute in Alabama that drove me. The path to college hasn't changed that much, but today's youth do have more opportunities than we did. Young people today have more resources, such as college and career counselors. More financial support is available in the form of scholarships and the HOPE and Pell grants. With greater opportunities, young people need to start the process of going to college before their senior year. When it was time for me to graduate, I was ready to leave high school and Milledgeville. As a result, I spent my summer following graduation speaking with locals who had attended college to get myself mentally prepared for the rigors of an advanced education—the goal was to level the playing field. I knew I had to better myself, and it would take more than a high school education. I drew on my grandfather's belief that things were going to get better and used it as fuel in my effort to be as prepared as possible for my postsecondary education.

Second Quarter (Matriculation, Marriage, and the Military)

Tuskegee Institute and the Making of a Man
My college years very quickly started the process of my becoming a man. I became the head drum major for the college band and was featured in the *Who's Who in American Colleges and Universities*. More importantly, going off to Tuskegee Institute in Alabama during the midst of the civil rights movement gave me the opportunity to be involved as a student activist. This gave me a chance to be in a leadership role with other students and staff. This opportunity allowed me to see that my grandfather's vision of things changing and getting better was a possibility that we could have a direct hand

in bringing to pass. Becoming an active participant in the struggle was a difficult decision. Doing so meant risking my future in the military if I was arrested and the possibility of being killed, like native Tuskegee student Sammy Younge, a classmate and student activist who later became a member of the Student Nonviolent Coordinating Committee. Sammy was murdered behind a gas station in Tuskegee, and there is no doubt that his murder was the result of his activism. But with the help of mentors like Dr. B. P. Phillips, dean of students, I was able to comfortably reconcile my involvement. Students today should still be engaged in bringing change to pass. This is especially true in politics. While our young people certainly possess the energy and courage to make a difference, they need to be well-versed in today's political climate. It doesn't always take an army; one person *can* make a difference—think President Nelson Mandela or President Barack Obama.

Initiating My Professional Path

A tremendous help to me was an academic advisor who owned a construction company in Tuskegee. I worked there part-time and even did some subcontracting for his company, which he wasn't able to do. While I was still in college, I also worked back home with former Georgia state representative Phillip Channel's construction company. We didn't have internships back then, but I made an opportunity for myself by working with these gentlemen—the equivalent to internships. This gave me the ability to have money and a car, things students did not have. Today, college internship is big; it's an apprenticeship, and you're getting paid to learn. College students should pursue internships, as this will give them the edge of experience when looking for their first job following graduation.

College ROTC Realities

There were two important things for me that came out of the Reserves Officers Training program in college: leadership training and the ability to manage. Participating in this program exposed me to an array of people and situations that set me up for the realities of being on active duty. ROTC's impact was clear when I began active duty. I was prepared and knew I could be successful. When I walked into my first duty station in Fort Lewis, Washington, I wasn't afraid to tackle tasks or was intimidated by those already there. Often, I encountered experienced officials from places like West Point, but I was ready and able to hold my own because of the training I received while at Tuskegee.

Meeting and Marrying My Mate

One day while hanging out between classes in my junior year, I spotted a young lady walking across campus with a friend of mine; her name was Nathalie Huffman, and she was from Birmingham, Alabama. I didn't know if the two of them were serious, but I said to myself, "I've been on campus for three years now, and she is the first female student that I really, really want to get to know." I eventually asked her for a date, and we went to a service at a chapel called Vespa, which was sort of a social. We dated for about a year and a half and got married during her senior year, but we remained in Tuskegee for a year before departing for my active duty in the army. Nathalie was very instrumental in my military transition and was with me every step of the way; she was what is viewed as a great officer's wife— very dutiful and helpful to me in achieving my goals. I'm not sure I would have been as successful as I was early on in my military career had Nathalie not been by my side. All military wives serve with their mates, but officers' wives are truly special. Moreover, Nathalie was the wife of a black officer, which posed other challenges. I believe that today's young couples should be individually grounded as we were before getting married. Use our situation as a guide regarding where you are and where you want to go in the future together. For example, early in our marriage, Nathalie said to me, "Floyd, if you will allow me to manage our finances, we will never have any financial problems." I didn't know what to think of that then, but I get it now. My wife and I made sure we shared everything. We never had a separate checking account, and we always operated from a budget. We had a savings account and an investment account. This is when we really started to become partners. It can create some challenges, but if the two of you are committed, you will be successful. You must properly think and act now so that what happens later in your marriage and with your children will be a result of your current thoughts and actions.

Active Duty Begins

Going into the army as a second lieutenant was one of the best things that could have happened to me. At the time, the military was still transitioning into ensuring that black officers had in place what they needed to be promoted (the military is set up for promotion based on your readiness). During the first year of my first official assignment working in my field of construction engineering, I applied for and was accepted to go to flight school to learn how to fly helicopters. Out of all the blacks in my flight class, I was the only one to graduate. The view by many blacks was that the higher-ups' goal was to root out as many blacks as possible during flight school; this made being a black aviator a big deal. I was extremely proud of having graduated flight school, and this period was followed by my first aviation assignment, my instructor pilot course, and finally, being assigned to Vietnam. I was on an assignment rotation during that year in Vietnam, and I commanded an engineer construction company in addition to flying and instructing. All these jobs were additional tools in my toolbox that allowed me to remain competitive (I needed to have a company command in order to advance). It was very important to serve as a commander in a combat situation. I even flew Ms. Black America around while in Vietnam. The kicker was that she was also from Birmingham, Alabama, my wife's hometown.

Climbing the Ladder Through Youth Outreach

A person should know the different stages of moving up the ladder in their chosen field. You need to know where you want to end up at the end of the day. I applied this methodology throughout my military career, a combination of planning and preparation so that when the opportunity came along, I wouldn't be passed over. I later started the ROTC program at Winston Salem State University in Winston

Salem, North Carolina, where I also coached running backs on the football team under the legendary coach William "Bill" Hayes, who was inducted into the Black College Football Hall of Fame in 2018. One of my players, former Dallas Cowboy Tim Newsome, whom I coached for three years, was also inducted into the Black College Football Hall of Fame in 2019. Coaching helped me to use my military experience to help my players develop a winning attitude; my philosophy was "Be a winner!" As we move through the different quarters in life, we should always find ways to work with young people. It could be athletics, civil or social organizations, or mentoring. I chose coaching; therefore, I did not get paid. Using football as a strategy to get young men in ROTC to become commissioned officers was a winning strategy. Some of those young men still thank me for what I did for them at Winston Salem State, offering their testimonies about how it impacted their professional and military careers. Life should be more than about us. It's about helping the whole, especially in our community.

Parenting

Parents need to be involved in their children's everyday lives. Our sons, Brian and Eric, are in the early years of their fourth quarter of life, and both are very successful. The former is a retired army colonel; the latter, an executive with Microsoft. Because all children naturally want their parents to be proud of them, you should always lead by example. Kids do what we do, not what we say. Our two sons saw me coaching football, and I coached them when they were in middle school. We took them to church and Sunday school instead of sending them. We got them involved in the affairs of the family. For instance, when they were in the first quarter of life and we hosted officers at our home for social events, they helped to serve the officers. They were afforded the chance during these socials to mingle with young men who had been successful in the first quarter of life and were now in the second quarter of life, working toward and achieving their goals. As children of a military family, our sons got a chance to live abroad, which exposed them to the lifestyles and cultures of people from all over the world. Having seen a very large variety of successful people in many walks of life, they later became self-starters. They wanted jobs; they wanted to take ownership of their advancement. After they finished college, my wife and I made a pact and "broke their plates," meaning, that they symbolically no longer had anything to eat at our home anymore. This meant that they were expected to forge their own way. They could come home anytime to visit and share a meal, but they couldn't come home again to stay. We did help them get a new car and made the first couple of payments for them when they graduated from college; this is vastly different from purchasing a car for a sixteen-year-old who has no idea which direction he or she will go. We also helped them get settled into their apartments once they started working. Because they have good jobs at Apple Computer in the case of Eric and as a second lieutenant in the army in the case of Brian, they are now raising their own children in much the same way. Thank God, to this day, we have not had one bit of trouble out of them. We have been really blessed with our children, and we are both so proud of them and happy for them. This kind of parenting stands to break generational curses. We have too many children today who are still living with Mom and Dad well beyond the third quarter of life without a good reason. Life really begins, at the beginning, with parents. As parents, we should give our all to our children from conception to age seventeen. At eighteen, they start being more independent, making decisions on their own and moving on. However, even as their parents, we should never stop being available for them.

Rising in Rank and Racing toward Retirement

During this time in my life, I was selected to command an engineer construction battalion at Fort Stewart, Georgia, under Major General Norman Schwarzkopf, who was later chosen to command the Desert Storm operations in the Middle East in the early 1990s. This position lasted for two years and gave me the opportunity to become more knowledgeable in the construction industry. More importantly, I gained tremendous experience managing and leading a major organization of over eight hundred soldiers. This work included vertical construction, overseeing building construction, and building roads and ranges. My tenure afforded me the opportunity to work in the Pentagon in Washington, DC, as well, a big step because of the level of responsibility involved. I came in as a lieutenant colonel and experienced two very defining moments in my career. The first event was when I was selected to attend Command and General Staff College, the equivalent of pursuing a master's degree. The second defining moment was being selected to attend the National War College, the equivalent of pursuing a doctorate, the highest level attainable in that branch of the service. Only a small percentage of students are selected to attend these two schools; to remain competitive, war college was a necessity. I was climbing the ladder fast and eventually achieved the rank of colonel. Like getting into Command and General Staff College and war college, a black officer achieving the rank of colonel is significant because only a small percentage of us are promoted to this rank. These two achievements coupled with going to flight school convinced me that I was on par with many of my counterparts. I also earned my master's degree in contracts and procurement management, a degree that the army paid for. A military officer's progression can be quite complicated if you don't stay on top of where you are at all times; there are a lot of moving parts. Several slack senior officers helped me to achieve my status and rank. They included Lieutenant General Joe Ballard, Major General Charles Williams, Major General Ernie Harrell, and Colonel William L. Mazych. General Williams and General Harrell are both Tuskegee graduates, and General Williams directly assisted me with achieving the ranks of lieutenant colonel and colonel and facilitated my appointment to serve on the Board of Trustees at Tuskegee University. The help they provided me is a powerful testament to the need for mentors in our life. If I didn't apply myself accordingly in the effort to advance throughout my military career, any one of the challenges associated with achieving success could have been a showstopper. Always be clear about your goals and what it's going to take to achieve them. No matter how talented a person is, the professional climb up the ladder is easier when you have networked and developed relationships with individuals who will vouch for you. In life, it's not always about what you know but who you know. You must get your foot in the door first to prove your worth. There's always someone right over your shoulder ready to take your place. Nevertheless, continue being a winner and continue to work hard and keep looking forward. It's all about being competent and understanding your chosen field. Though you must set goals to have a measure of success, you can't go through your professional career trying to do it alone. Find people up and down the ladder who believe in you and know what you're doing to assist you; it's virtually impossible to climb the ladder without some key people on your side.

LETTER TO GRANDSONS

Brandon, Braxton, Jamal, Oma, Opa, and Bakari

Train up a child in the way he should go; and
when he is old, he will not depart from it.

(Proverbs 22:6 King James Version)

My dearest grandsons,

What a joy it has been to watch you grow and mature! Oma (grandmother) and I, Opa (grandfather), have enjoyed being a part of every milestone and every achievement; your successes feel like our own as you have shared your experiences with us over the years, asking questions and listening to advices. As you read *Life: Four Quarters plus Overtime*, may you apply its wisdom to your own lives in ways that I cannot even conceive of at this time.

Jamal, you are the oldest. In your second quarter of life and as a fourth generation (Griffin) military man, I take great pride in your accomplishments. You have traveled abroad to many places while serving in the air force and have made sergeant, experiences, and achievements that many will never reach. Relish these experiences.

As you pursue your bachelor's degree, be thoughtful about how you will serve your fellow mankind in the coming years.

Brandon, you are also in your second quarter of life. As a third-generation Tuskegee University alumnus, you have much to offer the world as well. Your desire to become a medical doctor is noble—what better profession than healing! Internships abroad have afforded you the opportunity to experience medical practices around the world, experiences that you will take with you as you achieve your dreams.

Bakari, you are the artist of the bunch. From early childhood, your gift and compassion have shone brightly—what beauty you will bring to the world! In your second quarter of life, we are excited about the possibilities for you and where you will share your gifts after you finish school; your work and life will be an expression of who you are and how you perceive the world around you.

Braxton, as the youngest, you are in your second quarter of life and on your senior year in high school. Your athletic abilities and skills are incredible; you are a tremendous defensive back. Though we know that football is your main goal in life, please remember that there is life after the game. Your achievements in the Beta Club are exemplary; academic achievement will prepare you for all four quarters of life.

From a young age, you have all spent several weeks with us each summer; we are satisfied that we were able to instill the importance of an education in you through your attendance at Kids' University each year at Georgia College and State University.

Oma and I are 100 percent behind you in whatever you strive for throughout your lives; we hope that we have given you something to guide you in your endeavors. I encourage you to read *Life: Four Quarters plus Overtime,* turn down relevant pages, make notes in the margins—use a highlighter if you wish—and internalize its words. Use this book as a guidepost for your lives and pass it on to your future families, that they might benefit as well. Build upon this legacy that we are proud to leave you and become a legend in your right.

We are so proud to call you our grandsons.

With love,
Opa (grandfather) and Oma (grandmother)

Third Quarter (The End of Military Life and the Move Back Home)

Accepting Fate through Trust and Faith

Never say never. Around this time, I was twenty-three years into my military career with plans to stay in longer, but fate intervened and redirected my path to Milledgeville in my forty-sixth year. My parents were getting up in age and needed help with running the family business Slater's Funeral Home Inc. My sister, Delbra, had returned for the same reason, and together, we had a very successful business. When I left for college, my parents were not in the funeral business; they were in another business. Although, I had made up my mind never to return to Milledgeville to live, I decided it was time to change careers and return home to assist my parents and follow the current path God seemed to have me following. I was blessed to have obtained my goal of doing at least twenty years in the military and retiring with the rank of a colonel. Therefore, I had no regrets. We had moved fourteen times during my career, and I had held several positions. When I retired from the army in 1990, I put it behind me. My focus was now on obtaining the credentials needed to assist at the funeral home as vice president. First, I had to become qualified as a funeral professional, and I needed credentials to meet this goal. I retired in August and returned to Milledgeville in September to enter funeral service school for a year. Following that, I obtained my funeral director and embalmer license. I then took the state and national exams and passed. Finally, I completed my apprenticeship, which gave me the ability to preside over funeral services without the supervision of a funeral director. I became president of Slater's in 2005 and remained in this position until we sold the business in 2017. In order to oversee the business, I had to apply the same method used to advance my military career—setting goals, finding out what it takes to accomplish them, and applying myself accordingly served me well in obtaining my funeral service credentials—just as this method served me well in the army.

Transitioning through Patience and Perseverance

Coming back home was quite an adjustment. I had been gone for twenty-eight years, and it was like returning to a foreign land. This was especially true in the case of my wife, who was from another state. My major challenge was mastering the dynamics of working in the funeral business. I also had to deal with unwarranted, undeserved jealously and envy by some. A lot of people perceived my wife and me as thinking we were better than others. In the initial stages of running for a political position, I learned that there was a pecking order and that there were individuals who felt that you couldn't do anything without their permission. I accepted that getting to know the community and it getting to know me better was an advantageous reality. At this point, I proceeded to meet with key people in the community who were necessary to know once my campaigning began. For example, a local minister had me over to discuss my plans. He questioned whether it was a good idea for me to run for state senator and suggested that I might be in over my head. Before departing his office, I responded that I was going to run and win. I also told him, "If you want to be on the landing, you need to be on the takeoff." He later invited me back to his office, but this time, I reminded him that it was his turn to pay me a visit instead.

Spending quality time with people throughout the community also helped with some of the challenges of running for office. I frequently visited local churches, joined organizations like the NAACP and the SCLC, and even joined the Rotary Club (I became its first black member). I also served on the Board of Trustees at Georgia College and

State University. Making myself accessible to people was a good move. It helped prepare me for being in the senate and serving as mayor. Something that also made a tremendous difference was my supporting cast. My father was better by now, and he and my mother along with my sister, Delbra Waller, and my wife were very supportive.

During my campaigning time, my military training proved invaluable in helping me to handle myself when dealing with the public. The contents of a busy life are sometimes referred to in the military as glass balls. I had my hands full but juggling a lot of glass balls wasn't new to me. Juggling the balls is challenging because they're always in motion. The key is to never drop one of the glass balls. Because once they're broken, you can't put them back together again. This is just another way of saying, "Don't burn your bridges because you can't rebuild them." Glass balls are a good example of how I handled myself once I had discovered my purposes in life. Planning and preparing helped me to avoid poor performance because having goals and knowing what it takes to achieve them is 90 percent of the battle. This also helps to keep the stress level down. This also helps on a community level; decreasing stress can help the black community be more proactive and ensures greater success. There are too many stressful factors affecting our success; racism is just one example.

We must be more proactive in our approach to dealing with life to ensure generations of longevity. We have tremendous potential—we have the resources, we have the brainpower, and we have the skills. There is no reason we cannot be successful; all we have to do is apply ourselves in the manner prescribed to turn things around.

Fourth Quarter (Professional and Political Progression)

The Path to Politics
While serving as the vice president of Slater's Funeral Home, the president of Georgia Military College asked me to be the campus engineer. I agreed to do it for half a day at my leisure for a year and

then find a replacement. I also taught a management course for two quarters at Georgia College and State University. I worked in this capacity my first three years following my return to Milledgeville until I decided to get involved in politics and run for the state senate. It was a long shot that meant running against an incumbent who was also a doctor. Nevertheless, I laid the groundwork for the campaign and won. This was a historic moment; I was the first African American in modern times to win in a majority white rural legislative district. This was a big challenge because there were three of us in the Democratic primary, including the senator. The senator and I garnered the most votes and competed in a runoff, but I beat him with 54 percent of the vote, becoming the only African American in the state senate to represent a majority white district. I later decided to run for lieutenant governor of Georgia. We fell short, but I ran a good race, and two years later, I ran for mayor of Milledgeville. I defeated my opponent, Richard Bentley, by twenty-one votes, becoming the city's first black mayor. While serving as mayor, I operated in the same context as my military career—creating a plan of action for each initiative I implemented and assessing where my administration was along the way in each case until we met each goal. I also understood the magnitude of the position, and like my senatorial situation, I was the first black to oversee this district. How I administered authority and the will of Milledgeville residents would be weighed in a different way than my contemporaries. Therefore, I worked hard to honor those who made it possible for me to become mayor.

Measuring Success and What Success Looks Like
Every career is riddled with landmines, and I had to stay focused. I had to know where I was going and how to get there. Landmines are there most of the time because we allow them to be there. I would grade myself at the top of any scale as it relates to being successful. In 2002, the History Makers, a Chicago-based organization dedicated to recognizing leading African Americans in their chosen fields, decided to honor me, one of only two hundred individuals in the United States. As I entered overtime, I assessed my career and

personal accomplishments, such as being selected to serve on the board of directors for the National Center for Missing and Exploited Children and being awarded the James Wimberly Racial Error Award for Extraordinary Achievement. I concluded that if one can do the things that I have accomplished in the military, in politics, and in business and still be around to tell it, then you can consider yourself a success. I have worked in three different professions in the military, the funeral business, and politics, and there were some instances that could have sent me reeling. For example, I had a fifty-fifty record in politics, losing (and winning) half my races. But you must accept your losses and move on. I didn't stay focused on the times that I didn't win. I really had to apply this principle each time I had a new race to run because it was always in a majority white district or municipality; I knew it wasn't going to be easy winning as an African American candidate. I was quite clear on this fact and won anyway. When I first retired from the army and decided to get into politics, I was naive about what it was going to take for me to win. But through research and an assessment of each district, I was able to determine what it was going to take to at least give myself a good chance at success. So having won under these circumstances, half my political career at both the local and state levels, is a highly successful effort. Measuring success is based on everyone's goal and where they want to be at the end of the day. Each of us must decide what it is we want to accomplish if we want to measure our success. I wanted to be in construction, go into the army, and become an officer. When I retired from the military, I had a new career waiting for me in the family business back home in Milledgeville; this presented an opportunity to be successful in the overtime in an entirely new arena. In addition to my careers (and as a result of my successes in them), I am a member of the Winston-Salem State University Clarence E. "Big House" Gaines Athletic Hall of Fame and the Tuskegee University ROTC Hall of Fame. My memoirs, memorabilia, and professional papers are in the library of Georgia College and State University displayed as an exhibit in the W. J. Jr. Leadership Gallery. I wrote my autobiography, *Legacy to Legend: Winners Make It Happen*, and followed up with this book, making me an author. When reviewing my career, there's no doubt in my mind that my professional life was successful.

Teamwork Makes the Dream Work

I would never have achieved the success I have experienced if it weren't for my wife, Nathalie. She has been with me my entire professional career and through raising our boys. She really helped me keep those glass balls from hitting the ground. Nathalie made sure that I spent quality time with our sons, along with other mandatory domestic endeavors, and I was extremely fortunate that I was never away from my family during my twenty-three years in the military for more than a year. My time in Vietnam was the only period that I was gone extensively. There were instances when I would travel during temporary travel duty for three or four days at a time in the latter years of my military career, but for the most part, I was home each night. As I approached the fourth quarter of life, we would find ways to stay connected to our sons and grandchildren. They lived in other cities, but we would get together during holidays and family reunions. We have four biological grandsons who would visit during the summer, and we always got them involved in Children's College at Georgia College and State University. It was like a summer camp, and they enjoyed being a part of it and meeting other children from around Milledgeville. We liked exposing them to this and other activities, but one of the things that we were very intentional about was not trying to run our sons' lives. It's very important to reach a happy medium in this. Naturally, it depends on where your children live. It's easier to interact with your children and grandchildren in an ongoing way if they live in the same city as you. Today our son Brian is a retired colonel after thirty years in the army. He is living in Alabama and is getting ready for his next career move. Eric, the younger of the two, is an executive with Microsoft and resides in the Atlanta area. I can't give my wife enough credit for helping them reach their goals, just as she did with me. I'm glad that I allowed her to do what she did best, keep the family on track. We had our challenges as do all married couples, and we don't profess to having been perfect. But our love, faith, and commitment to each other created a collaboration that exemplifies the adage "Teamwork makes the dream work."

Overtime—Seventy Plus (Enjoying the Golden Years and Leaving a Legacy)

Retirement Is for Relaxation and Restoration
I've only been in overtime for four years, but our whole lives up through the fourth quarter should be spent planning for overtime. The Bible says that this period is special and is possible. You shouldn't wait until the fourth quarter to plan for overtime; there are several things that you should being doing during each quarter. Most importantly, take care of your health. Do everything that you can—eat right, get enough rest and exercise, and make sure you visit your doctor for a physical every year. Black men should be getting their prostates checked as their doctors recommend, as prostate cancer is a leading cause of death among black men. I have encouraged my sons to get their prostates checked every year beginning at age fifty. It's not known by a lot of people other than my family circle, but I had prostate cancer. Fortunately, doctors caught it very early during an annual physical, and I went through five weeks of treatment. Today, I'm cancer-free. According to my studies, most black men are going to get prostate cancer at some stage of their life, so they need to stay on top of their screening (during my time as a helicopter pilot, they would routinely check our prostates).

Another area that needs to be focused on is retirement income. If you want to retire between sixty-five and seventy, then you need to have a plan as early as possible. Remember, in most cases, you can't live off social security; you will need additional financial resources. Overtime should be about relaxing, minimizing stress, doing what you want to do, and giving back to your family and friends in a different way. This should be the time when you can do the things you always thought about but couldn't because of the hustle and bustle of life during the previous quarters. I was able to write this book about life because I'm in overtime and had the kind of time I needed to create it. I'm also volunteering in the community on several things including the Baldwin County Charter System Foundation of Excellence. This foundation was established by the Baldwin County School System in order to provide resources for children who can't be supported with tax dollars, like scholarships or events. My wife and I have established the Floyd Griffin and Nathalie Griffin endowed scholarship fund to support this foundation, and I currently serve as the chairman of this board. I also previously served on the Tuskegee Institute board for seven years. While serving on this board, we established the Floyd and Nathalie Griffin Family Endowed Scholarship. We have always enjoyed traveling and seeing new things, so my wife and I have a bucket list of places we plan to go. Nathalie is a big Atlanta Braves fan, and I enjoy taking her to several home games each baseball season. Having a solid plan during the first four quarters of my life has made it possible to enjoy my wife, children, grandchildren, and family friends and to help out with assistance and advice to young people whenever possible.

Oral and Written History as a Frame of Reference
I recently received the Middle Georgia Fisk University Alumni Leontine Espy Award of Excellence. I and the other four recipients are all in the overtime of life. Society should take advantage of the years of experience of overtimers because they bring with them over seventy years of invaluable experience. It doesn't matter who they are or what their nationality, race, or socioeconomic status is—they have a wealth of knowledge they can pass on. Younger people should spend more time drawing from seniors' lives and learning from them. I was a little negligent when it came to seeking this knowledge from more overtimers, and I wish I had spent more time with my mom and dad and aunts and uncles just talking about life. It would have made it easier to write this book. You can find out some amazing things just by asking questions. Black people need to get back to a better understanding of our ancestors and history. Each person has an autobiography in them, a lifetime of experience and wisdom to

pass on to their children and family members, anyone who wants to learn from them. It's important that we capture and preserve our history to serve as a reference for generations coming behind us. A lot of our experiences are good ones, and how success was achieved needs to be shared. Even the experiences that weren't so good can serve as a resource so that future generations won't make similar mistakes. I was blessed to be a resource for my older son when he was rising in rank. He would confer with me on what he needed to do along the way to be a colonel. Having his father (along with other elders) that he could call on smoothen the way for him and made success possible. The same thing happened with our younger son as he charted his course and his career. Nathalie and I are now guiding our goddaughter in the same way, as she navigates the third quarter of her life. This should be what we're doing so that our children don't have to go up the rough side of the mountain. They can go up the smooth side.

Life Is Not Over until It's Over
Overtime should be treated as a continuation of life. You should be doing the things you want to do, instead of simply sitting down and waiting for the Lord to call you home. We all are going to have health-related challenges in overtime. Some will be slightly significant, and others may be extremely so, but we shouldn't be sitting around waiting to die. Understand that life is not over until it's over. The day I retired and sold the business, I got up the next morning and got out of the house, determined to do something. This is now my routine every morning; my day begins around 8:00 a.m. with a cup of tea at Starbucks in Milledgeville, followed by meet and greet at Burger King, where I chitchat with close friends. Then around 10:00 a.m., I move on to important endeavors until about 1:00 p.m. Next, I return home, and I don't leave again unless there's an evening function that I plan to attend. Once I'm home, I read, look at a little television, take care of honey do list, and converse with my wife until it's time to retire for the day. I enjoy the relaxing part, but I'm still active, just in a different way and at a slower pace.

LETTER TO MY WIFE

My dearest Nathalie,

How can I tell you what you mean to me? There will never be enough words.

"Who can find a virtuous woman? For her price is far above rubies. The heart of her husband doth safely trust in her, so that he shall have no need of spoil. She will do him good and not evil all the days of her life" (Proverbs 31:10–12 KJV).

I found that woman my best friend, my confidante, my solid rock. You've been my partner for over five decades through college, the military, and my business and political careers. You have raised our two sons with a love that only a mother can give and a faith that is strong and unwavering. You are a loving grandmother to our four grandchildren and two step-grandchildren and have extended that same love to our goddaughter.

We have seen babies learn to walk and talk, school years with projects and field trips, college and weddings, the birth of grandchildren—all while you remained steadfast and loyal. Through good and bad times, you have been my shoulder to lean on, a listening ear, warm arms to hold me close. You make all things better.

Oh, how wonderful it is to know that you share my sentiments, recorded in my autobiography, *Legacy to Legend: Winners Make It Happen*, when you said, "Floyd is my very best friend. We can sit in a room together and not say a word. But each knows what the other is thinking. We have both been blessed, and we are indeed thankful each day. I look forward to growing older together." Well, my dear— we are there now, and I love you more with every passing day. You are the blessing that I thank God for the most!

Your dearest Floyd

MY HOPE FOR THE READERS

As a reader, you are in one of the quarters in this book; you should be striving to make it to overtime. You should be planning your life to get to that point. It's a beautiful thing to live four quarters plus overtime knowing that you've done the best you could for yourself, your family, and your community. I pray that you will continue to have a desire to give back in a way that will keep you focused and moving. Most of all, I hope that you have or will develop a plan to move through the earlier quarters of life to ensure that you can enjoy your own overtime. I pray that your life is as fulfilling as mine and that your journey will be one marked by memorable moments worth reflecting on by you and deserving of being shared with those coming behind you. It's my hope that each of you will write your memoirs to pass on your legacy to the next generation of your family. Enjoy your life and Godspeed.

I can do all things through Christ which strengtheneth me.

(Philippians 4:13 King James Version)

ABOUT THE AUTHOR

The Honorable Floyd L. Griffin Jr.
Former mayor, City of Milledgeville
Former Georgia state senator
Colonel, US Army (retired)

At different times in his life, Floyd L. Griffin Jr. has been a cadet, Vietnam helicopter pilot, army colonel, football coach, professor, businessman, state senator, mayor, and author. Throughout his life of change and challenges, Floyd Griffin has always been dedicated to public service.

Griffin is former co-owner of Slater's Funeral Home Inc. in Milledgeville, Georgia. He served on the board of trustees of his alma mater Tuskegee University in Tuskegee, Alabama. He currently serves on the board of visitors at Georgia College and State University in Milledgeville, Georgia. Griffin was inducted into the Winston-Salem State University Clarence E. "Big House" Gaines Athletic Hall of Fame and Tuskegee University's ROTC Hall of Fame. His oral history video is included as a permanent record of the HistoryMakers Collection at the Library of Congress. The Floyd L. Griffin Jr. papers are held by the Ina Dillard Russell Library Special Collections at Georgia College and State University.

In 1994, Griffin did what political experts said was impossible. He literally stormed into the political scene and defeated an incumbent Georgia state senator. The victory made Griffin the first African American in modern times to be elected in a rural legislative district containing a majority of white voters. In 2000, Griffin continued to do what political experts said was impossible by becoming the first African American mayor of the Old Capitol City of Milledgeville, Georgia.

The honorable Floyd Griffin served as senator of Georgia's Twenty-Fifth District for two terms. In the Georgia Senate, Griffin was chairman of the Interstate Cooperation Committee and served on the Defense and Veteran's Affairs, Health and Human Services, Higher Education, Local and State Government Operations, and the powerful Rules Committees. In 1998, Griffin was candidate for lieutenant governor of Georgia. His candidacy for lieutenant governor made him the first African American to run for that office in the twentieth century. Griffin was elected mayor of the city of Milledgeville for the term 2002–2006. He was the sixty-seventh mayor to serve. In 2009, Griffin published his autobiography, *Legacy to Legend: Winners Make It Happen*.

In 1967, he entered the United States Army. In Vietnam, Griffin served as a helicopter pilot, instructor pilot, aviation platoon leader, and commander of a construction engineer company. After combat service, he commanded an engineer battalion under General Norman Schwarzkopf and was later promoted to the rank of colonel and then served on the army staff at the Pentagon.

Floyd Griffin has also worked as an educator. At Wake Forest University, he served as an assistant professor of military science. He was the director of ROTC at Winston-Salem State University, where he coached the football team's backfield as they won two conservative college championships. Griffin has served as a part-time instructor at the Georgia College and State University School of Business.

Griffin holds a bachelor of science in building construction degree from Tuskegee University and master of science in contract and procurement management degree from Florida Institute of Technology. Griffin holds an associate of science in funeral service degree from Gupton-Jones College. He is a graduate of the Army Command and General Staff College and the National War College.

After twenty-three years of service in the United States Army, Griffin returned to his hometown of Milledgeville, Georgia.

Griffin is a member of a number of organizations, which include Sigma Pi Phi, the American Legion, Prince Hall of Free and Accepted Masons, Nations War College Association, a life member of the Omega Psi Phi, and 100 Black Men Organization of Milledgeville and Baldwin County. He has served as a member of the board of trustees of several community organizations, to include Georgia College and State University Foundation's Board of Trustees, Georgia Military College Board of Trustees, the National Conference of Black Mayors' Board of Directors, and as the president of the Georgia Conference of Black Mayors. In 2002, he was presented the James Wimberly Racial Barrier Breaker Award for the extraordinary achievement of being the first African American mayor of Milledgeville, Georgia. Griffin was also chosen and saluted as one of the 2002 recipients of the National History Makers in Chicago, Illinois. He also served on the Board of Directors of the National Center for Missing and Exploited Children in Alexandria, Virginia.

Griffin is a Milledgeville native and is married to the former Nathalie Huffman, also a Tuskegee graduate. They have two sons, also Tuskegee University graduates, and four grandsons.

CPSIA information can be obtained
at www.ICGtesting.com
Printed in the USA
BVHW032357171019
561407BV00001B/2/P

9 781796 061550